ARABIAN NIGHTS & ARABIAN NIGHTS

Traditional tales from a thousand and one nights, Contemporary tales for adults

Clive Johnson

labyrinthe

Labyrinthe Press
www.labyrinthepublishers.com

Labyrinthe Press
Leigh-on-Sea, United Kingdom
www.labyrinthepublishers.com

Publisher's Note: This is a work of fiction. Names, characters, places,
and incidents are a product of the author's or original storyteller's
imagination. Locales and public names are sometimes used for at-
mospheric purposes. Any association with actual people, living or
dead, or to organisations, events, or institutions, is unintentional.

Book Layout ©2013 BookDesignTemplates.com
Cover illustration © CanStockPhoto/nasir1164
Cover format by Jacqueline Abromeit
Distributed by Ingram

British Library Cataloguing in Publication Data
Arabian Nights & Arabian Nights/ Clive Johnson. —1st ed.
ISBN 978-0-9932029-6-4 (Print edition)
ISBN 978-0-9932029-7-1 (Electronic edition)
Also available as an Audible digital audiobook.

Please note that the traditional tales in this book (the first chapter in each part) are suitable for older children, although parental guidance is advised. All other stories are intended for adult readers, and are not suitable for children.

In the same series:

Fairy Stories & Fairy Stories–
Traditional tales for children, Contemporary tales for adults

CONTENTS

Introduction

With its countless stories of wish-granting jinn, flying carpets, fantastical treasure troves, and villains and misfits, it's no wonder that tales from the *One Thousand and One Nights* have excited the imaginations of countless readers since they were first introduced to Europe in the eighteenth century. Excepting the exquisite poetry of *The Qur'an* and the great epics from Hindu scripture, the *Nights* are supreme among Oriental literature.

The diversity of subjects that feature in this great treasury of tales is staggering—political satire and religious allegory, petty criminality and bold provocation, ingenious automatons and deserted cities. The stories tell of penniless beggars and wealthy merchants, of men of state and men of low-life, of treacherous women and heroines of high repute.

The tales vary greatly in their length–some being novellas reaching to more than one hundred pages each, others extending to barely a few sentences. There is an interweaving between some of the tales, and all are set within the shell of a single frame story. Furthermore, some of the stories are cast within even deeper levels of framing narrative.

The main frame story itself raises questions about sexual politics, and quickly sets in motion a tantalising series of cliff-hangers. This presents the storytelling of Scheherazade–the beautiful and clever daughter of the chief vizier to a tyrannical ruler–as a strategy to save both her own life, and the lives of all women whose lives are threatened by the jealous sultan.

The tales have their origins in at least four heart-lands of ancient civilisation–Persia, China, India, and Egypt. Scheherazade herself, meanwhile, is presented as representing women of different cultures–she speaks Arabic, has a Persian name, and her stories often display an Indian narrative style.

In relating the tales, a wide range of narrative styles are employed, including "historical epics, wisdom literature, fables, cosmological fantasy, pornography, mystical devotional tales, chronicles of low life, rhetorical debates and masses of poetry", as the historian and novelist Robert Irwin puts it in his Companion to the *Nights*[1].

The stories don't follow a common pattern–some teach moral lessons, some satirise political aristocracy; some provoke debate, while others seem to have no purpose other than to entertain. In some, heroes and heroines earn rich rewards for their virtuous actions; in others, seemingly unjustified twists of fate are described, with mischievous characters being rewarded, and welldoers coming to unhappy endings.

It's not agreed how many tales comprise the canon of the *Nights*. Indeed, the reference to one thousand and one nights in the title may simply be meant to indicate a very large number.

Some of the tales that are most commonly included are thought to originate from the tenth and eleventh centuries, while the frame story itself seems to have been inspired by the *Hazar Afsanah* ("*A thousand legends*")–an ancient Persian book of fairytales that first appeared in Arabic about 850 CE.

The authenticity of other tales is uncertain. Notably, some of the better known stories (*Ali Baba and the Forty Thieves*, the voyages of *Sinbad the Sailor*, and *Aladdin*) have not been traced to ancient manuscripts. Rather, these are often assumed to be creations

---

[1] Irwin, R. (1994), *The Arabian Nights: A Companion*, Allen Lane, p2.

of Antoine Galland, the brilliant French orientalist who first popularised the *Nights* in Europe with his translation, *Les mille et une nuits.* Galland alleges that the stories came to him from a Syrian source, but their origin remains unauthenticated.

While there's considerable overlap in the contents of the English translations of the *Nights* that appeared during the nineteenth century, the story details vary between these. Similarly, the list of tales that are included in these voluminous renditions vary considerably.

I don't believe that the provenance of such stories really matters–they certainly incorporate elements of older tales, and are faithful to the spirit of earlier writings in their styles, settings, and uses of motifs.

In my retellings of the stories included in this volume, I've not been concerned to follow what are considered to be accurate translations. This free-licence approach seems permissible to me, considering that the original meaning will at any rate often be lost when an interpreter attempts to transcribe from Arabic into English.

Rather, I have focused on respecting the general storylines and messages of the texts. I have adapted some details, while drawing from the three main English translations–Edward Lane's bowdlerized 1859 edition, John Payne's nine volumes (published in

1882), and the well-known 1885 collection of Sir Richard Burton.

For this volume, I've selected stories that address varying themes, as well as ones that demonstrate differing perspectives of the storytellers who related them. Some of the stories that I've chosen are well-known; others less so.

In the contemporary stories that parallel the traditional tales, I've attempted to maintain one or more aspects of the plotline, moral or meaning that feature in the originals.

This said, there is no single, comprehensive interpretation for the original tales, and commentators of the *Nights* don't always share common perspectives. For example, Scheherazade is seen by some writers as being a prototypical feminist who stands up to the tyranny of one man, but is portrayed as a mysterious challenger to the patriarchy of the Abrahamic faiths by others[2].

The brief reflections that I offer at the end of each tale on possible ways for interpreting the stories do not pretend to be authoritative or exhaustive. Neverthe-

---

[2] See, for example, the differing perspectives taken by the feminist writers Ethel Johnston Phelps and Nawal El Saadawi (in Malti-Douglas, F, *Scheherazade Feminist*, in Marzolph, U. (ed.) (2006), *The Arabian Nights Reader*, Wayne State University Press, pp 347-64).

less, I hope that these might help to stimulate thinking on what the original storytellers might have intended.

Of course, storytelling is a dynamic endeavour—every telling of a story is a unique performance that plays to an always new audience. Often, a storyteller seeks to enlighten and educate, but always he or she intends to engage and entertain.

The ability of tales from the *Nights* to repeatedly engage and entertain is perhaps why they have endured over several centuries. I hope that their wonderful depictions of exotic lands and dome-and-turret-crowned city skylines, their gripping plot lines, and mystery and magic will continue to bring pleasure and fresh wonder to adults who may be familiar with many of them, as well as to younger readers who may be coming to them for the first time.

The City of Brass

It is told that during the period of the Commander of the Faithful Abdulmelik ben Merwan, the great caliph was once entertained in conversation with his advisers at his palace in Damascus. Their debates ranged widely, but they settled upon discussing the tradition of Solomon, son of David (peace be upon him), upon whom Allah on High bestowed dominion over men, jinn, birds, beasts, and reptiles.

The gathered men reasoned that never in history had The Almighty ordained that such authority be accorded to any man such as he.

It was said that Solomon used to imprison jinn, marids and satans in vessels of copper. These were secured with molten lead, marked with the king's seal, and were then thrown into the sea.

One of the caliph's advisers, Talib ben Sehl–also known as 'Seeker of the Treasures'–related a story told by his grandfather that had in turn been passed on to him by his own father.

The story concerned the fate of a ship's crew who had set sail for the island of Sicily. Strong winds prevailed against the travellers, causing them to be driven far from their course and onto shores close to the great mountains of the Lord God, The Most High.

When daylight came, the local people–who presented themselves fully naked–greeted the marooned assembly. These people were not accustomed to the Arab tongue, save for their king. The king gave welcome to the shipwrecked men, and questioned their story. No Arab brethren had set foot in this land before, but they were received with the utmost kindness, and hosted for a full three days.

On the fourth day, the men came with their host to watch fishermen who were engaged in their trade on the shore. After a considerable struggle, one drew in his net, revealing in his catch a vessel of copper, which was sealed with molten lead.

Without appearing to be surprised, the fisherman broke open the vessel, wherefrom a tall plume of blue smoke burst forth, and from which then came a terrible voice.

"I repent, I repent! Pardon me, great prophet of God! I will never fail you again!" sounded the voice.

The smoke twisted and rose swiftly like a whirl-wind, quickly changing shape to reveal the figure of a grotesque giant, whose head reached as high as the mountaintops. Just as quickly as it had appeared, the hideous figure vanished.

The mariners were terrified, but the king told them to not be afraid. He said that his guests had witnessed the sight of one of the jinn that had been imprisoned by the great King Solomon, and that the discovery of these vessels close to the shore was not uncommon.

The caliph was enthralled by Talib's story. "Glory be to Allah!" he cried, "Surely, our mighty ancestor Solomon was given a holy dominion!"

One of the others present, En Nabigheh edh Dhub-yani, then offered: "Talib has spoken well. And it is said that The Almighty instructed Solomon to rule with a firm and strenuous hand–to be benevolent to the faithful, but to take away the freedom of those who were not." En Nabigheh continued, "So it was that he would imprison demons in these vessels of copper, and throw them into the sea."

"It's my desire to see one or more of these vessels," proclaimed the caliph.

"Great Master, this you may have!" replied Talib, "And without Your Majesty needing to leave your kingdom!"

Talib, who had read from the *Book of Hidden Treasures*, advised that the caliph should send word to his brother, Abdulaziz ben Merwen, asking him to write to Mousa ben Nuseir, who was the governor of Morocco. He should ask Mousa to order a caravan to be sent to the shore that lies beyond the mountains at the edge of his kingdom, where he might retrieve as many of such vessels as the caliph desired.

Satisfied with this proposal, the caliph appointed Talib as his messenger, affording him many camels and provisions for his journey. The caliph wrote to his brother as had been proposed, and also prepared a letter for Mousa, who was viceroy in North Africa.

Talib went first to Cairo, where the caliph's brother entertained him. He was conveyed to Upper Egypt, where the emir Mousa lived. Mousa, in turn, was happy to greet the caliph's messenger and to accept his master's command.

Mousa assembled his officers, who consulted on how best to execute the plan. One urged that the emir send for Sheikh Abdussemed, son of Abdulcuddous es Semoudi. The sheikh was known to be a wise man, widely travelled and familiar with the deserts and other waste worlds. Duly, the elderly sheikh was summoned to the emir's presence, and was entreated to join the expedition.

"I hear and obey!" responded the sheikh, "But beware that the road that we must face is long and difficult, hiding many perils."

The sheikh advised that the journey would take at least two years and several months more, as well as an equal amount to return. But he asserted his faith in The Almighty, Whom he declared would protect the party from every adversity.

The emir prepared to leave, appointing his son to rule in his stead, lest the Nazarenes attempt to cause mischief during his absence from office. One thousand camels and two thousand horse were readied.

The camels were laden with food and a store of gugglets, which the sheikh advised would more reliably hold water in the fierce desert heat than would mere water skins.

The expedition then set off along the route that the sheikh advised, following the shoreline, where there were many places for rest. This was a path known to the sheikh, who had travelled the route before.

As they journeyed, the entourage passed by many ruins and encountered the territory that had once belonged to the Greek king of Alexandria. Crossing far across desert lands, they eventually sighted lofty mountains in the distance, which towered as high as the sky.

One morning, following a full night of travelling, the sheikh found himself in a place that he didn't know. Since the sky had been obscured the previous night, he had been unable to rely on navigating by the stars, as was his habit.

The emir entreated him to guide the party back to where they had gone astray, but the sheikh advised that they had detoured too far. And so, following the emir's command, the travellers resolved to continue to follow the direction that they were taking, trusting Allah to bring them to a safe destination.

After some time, the party came across a calm sea of sand—a level plain that stretched for many miles. A tall black edifice came into view in the far distance, enveloped with what they assumed to be thick smoke, which was billowing high into the sky.

Anxious to gain a closer view of the mysterious sight before them, the caravan diverted still further from its course until they stood before what they could now see was a mighty castle. The magnificent structure was built of black stone, and was crowned by an imposing dome, which was one thousand cubits high.

Dominating the wall that they now faced, and approached by one thousand steps, was a gigantic door of gleaming China steel. Mousa marvelled at what he saw, but was curious to know why no living creature appeared to be about the castle.

"Praise be to Allah, Almighty Creator, The Lord of Heaven and Earth!" cried the sheikh. "It is He alone who has delivered us from this frightful desert!"

The emir questioned why the sheikh was so confident about their deliverance. The sheikh replied that his father had told him a story that had been related by his grandfather, who had once come to this palace and from hence to the City of Brass, from where they must take the coastal road to reach their destination.

Before continuing their journey, the emir and his companions determined to explore the marvellous castle. Its gates opened up easily to reveal a giant hall, whose ceiling was supported by lofty columns as high as the tallest cedar tree. Its walls contained porticoes, each decorated with mosaics of brilliantly coloured stone.

Ahead of them was a cascade of steps, fashioned from polished marble, which led through a doorway into another room. Above the doorway, the men noticed a large tablet, inscribed with gold letters. The sheikh, who was conversant in many languages, recognised the alphabet and so read the inscription for the benefit of his companions.

"You follow after those whose foregoing bids you warning of the course that you tread. You have passed by the dwellings of folks who lived well for a time, but who were fated to suffer the power that overcomes all. Here in this place you see forgotten evidence of earthly lords that once dallied here, but whose lordship is now reduced to dust. Death took them at their appointed hour. For what they had laboured, death would not accept as payment. And so, they hastily laid down the life that they once knew. Taking their fateful course, a path avoided by only a glorious few."

The emir was deeply troubled when he heard these strange verses, prostrating himself, and crying aloud for salvation from his Lord. "Truly there is no God but Allah, The Great!" he exclaimed. "Come, let us venture further, that we might marvel at the majesty of this place!"

The adventurers then came upon a further door, over which hung another tablet, which was also inscribed with gold. The sheikh related what he saw written there:

"So many have dallied in halls lined with gold, then taken their leave and proceeded on their way. The change of fortune that befell those who chose to stray is clear to see. They ate, they drank, and they enjoyed delights of many kinds. But now dust is their only sustenance for all time."

As the sheikh finished his reading, the emir fell to the ground to pray once more. "Truly ours is the greatest Creator, Who decrees a mighty purpose for all!" Deeply affected by what he had heard, the emir ushered his fellow travellers still further toward the castle's heart.

They observed four hundred tombs, and stood in amazement beneath the mighty dome. Sighting an inscription on the headstone of the greatest tomb, the sheikh read once more:

"So many things did indeed pass before my sight! I drank fine wine, and gnawed on rich meat, listening to songs anew. I gave commands, and conquered a few. I dallied with so many maids, whose secrets others never knew. But my hope of salvation passed away–my ignorance would not save me. Beware, you too will soon make food for the dust, lest you heed the warnings–as you must!"

Filled with awe, Mousa and his companions wept before the mighty tomb. They then advanced still further, coming before a golden-canopied pavilion. The pavilion had eight doors made of sandalwood, whose precious surface was emblazoned with gold, and ruby studs, and stars of glimmering silver.

Above the first door was written the warning:

"That which I left behind I made without generous design. Fate overtook me, as it will all humankind. Once I lived contentedly and saw my prosperity grow. Never did I give to others of my kin. One day I was stricken. Death came quickly–my troops could not help me. I took the road that all must follow, and soon a gravedigger was brought for me. Now the companions on my journey are my sins and my crimes. I am bereft of choice but to await God on His Judgement Day. Do not be deceived by what you see. Stay strong in the faith, and be not led astray."

Filled with remorse and sadness, the emir wept until his tears wetted his garments. At length, praising God, he led his party into the pavilion.

Here, they espied another tablet, adorned with still more verses that were written in gold. The inscription shone above them, demanding attention. The sheikh revealed its message:

"In the Name of The One, The Eternal God, unto Whom there is none alike! Be warned those who come here to take heed of what you see. Judge well the products of time and the changing circumstances of fortune. Let not the attractions of the world seduce you, nor its lies lead you into vanity. All that you have is but a loan, and soon the borrower will demand back what is rightfully His!"

The sheikh's voice began to tremble as he read these words, but he gathered himself, and continued:

"Take heed from my example. Once I had a wife and one thousand daughters, who were married to kings who had hearts as strong as lions. My palace harboured untold treasures; my days numbered one thousand years. My people and I dwelt here in leisure until the judgement of the One Provider and Destroyer devastated our land with tempest and hurricane. His vengeance came quickly upon us, every day taking two more souls, until all but a few of our company had perished.

"My soldiers were no match for the terrors that were let loose on us. My chamberlain could offer no treasure sufficient to allay the judgement of The Almighty. All the wealth that I had accumulated could ransom not one day of my life. Ultimately, I succumbed to my fate, to bear the infliction decreed upon me. And now in this grave rest I.

"Know that I am Koush, son of Sheddad, son of Aad the Greater, who once held dominion over this earth. When I saw what was happening, I summoned a writer to inscribe the warnings that you now read. Beware the chasm that faces all who put their trust in worldly riches and cavalry of men. Beware the changes of fortune that are always close at hand!"

Upon hearing the fate of this once mighty people, the emir could not fight back his tears. Prostrating himself before Allah once more, he shouted praise to his God.

Then he rose and observed a table made of yellow onyx, on which were inscribed the words:

"One thousand kings blinded of the right eye, and one thousand blinded of the left, and one thousand more who were sound of both eyes, have all taken leave from here to wander in their tombs."

The emir wrote down everything that the sheikh had translated. The party then prepared to depart from the castle. They left everything in its stead, save for the table, which they added to their stock.

For three days they journeyed on, until they sighted a hill on which stood a brass statue of a horseman. He held aloft a lance of startling brightness, upon which were engraved the words:

"O thou that comes here, if thou knows not the road to the Brazen City, rub the hand of this warrior, and he will revolve and eventually come to rest. Take the direction that he then faces, and journey on without hesitation. This straight path will bring you to the city that you seek."

The emir followed this instruction. No sooner had he rubbed the horseman's hand, than the statue started to revolve at great speed. Eventually it came to rest, facing a direction that was opposed to the caravan's current course.

The expedition proceeded along the path that the horsemen indicated—a well-beaten track—until after some days they came upon a pillar of brass, in which was embedded a fearsome creature.

The figure had two giant wings and four arms—two of a human's kind, and two of a lion's, with claws of iron. The creature had hair like the swaying tail of a horse, and its fierce eyes appeared to be blazing like coals. It had a third eye in the midst of its forehead, which appeared as if it were that of a lynx, burning with fire.

"All glory to my God!" shouted the figure, "Who has judged me, and Whose punishment I must now suffer!"

The group were greatly troubled by what they saw, and turned to flee. The emir asked the sheikh what it was that they had seen, but the sheikh could not answer him. So, the emir entreated him to approach the figure and question its history, observing that it could not move and so should not harm him.

Faithful to his Lord, the sheikh approached the creature, asking its name and its story.

"I am an Afreet of the jinn," replied the creature. "I am named Dahish, son of El Aamesh. I am confined at the pleasure of The Almighty.

"My story is strange. I was charged with guarding a powerful idol, which was served by the master of the kings of the sea. He was a king of great power and prowess, a ruler over all the warriors of the jinn, who answered to his every whim. All were beneath my command, and were rebels of Solomon, son of David, on whom be peace! I used to enter into the hollow body of the idol, from which I would command the jinn.

"The king's daughter adored this idol, and would often prostrate herself before it. She was the most charming of women, and was made known to Solomon, who sent a message to her father that she might become his wife.

"Solomon furthermore entreated him to destroy his idol, and to affirm his faith in The One Almighty. In turn, he promised a share of all that was his. However, should the king refuse, Solomon threatened to come upon him with an irresistible force.

"The king was very proud, but consulted with his viziers on the nature of Solomon's demand. His viziers advised that Solomon would not be able to realize his threat, since the marids and the jinn worked for the idol's favour, and the power contained in the idol would surely give him victory. They recommended that the king seek counsel from the idol, to ascertain its guidance–whether to take up arms against Solomon, or to concede to his request.

"The king took on sackcloth and made sacrifices of men before the idol, submitting himself to its oracle. The idol proclaimed that it knew all, and that the king's armies would prevail against Solomon.

"Hardened of heart, the king resolved to face Solomon in battle, and duly sent a messenger to him, to give notice of his decision.

"Solomon quickly raised a mighty army of men–jinn, and beasts of the land and the air. Jinn and marids were assembled together from all around. His viziers called up an army of one million men, all fully armoured.

"Then Solomon mounted his magic carpet and rose into the air, with the birds flying alongside and above him, and the beasts of the land following below. There he proclaimed, 'Behold, I am Solomon. Prepare to defend yourself, or else confess the true faith!'

"Mighty Solomon made clear his warning: "Fool will you be if you attempt to defend yourself here, for Allah the Almighty has given me the command of the winds, and I will come swiftly to you and suffer you as an example to others."

"Still, the king continued to ignore Solomon's warning, calling on the one million jinn under his command, and the marids and satans from the islands of the sea that were under his dominion.

"Solomon gathered his hosts ready to do battle, dividing his beasts into two parts, one wing bearing on the right and one on the left. Then he commanded them to rip their adversaries' horses in sunder. He gave orders to the birds to use their beaks to pluck out the eyes of the enemy, and to accost their faces with their strong wings. Then Solomon, enthroned on his carpet, commanded the wind to carry him aloof, such that he might survey his armies around him.

"Battle raged fiercely for two full days, filling every acre of an immense plain.

"On the third day, disaster came upon me, whereupon I experienced God's judgement. I had advanced to meet Solomon's vizier Ed Dimiryat in single combat, but he came upon me breathing fire and flame. At first, I avoided his attack and returned a blow to him, but his fury overcame me, commanding every power in his charge.

"I continued to wage battle with Ed Dimiryat, but at length my labour wearied me, and I was taken captive. I was brought before Solomon himself, who hollowed out the pillar that you see before you and fixed me in it. I was then brought to this place, which is my prison until the Day of Judgement."

The emir and his crew marvelled at what they had heard. "In truth," asserted the emir, "There is no God but Allah! Solomon was truly gifted with a mighty charge!"

The sheikh asked the jinn whether he knew of any Afreets that had been imprisoned in vessels of copper at the time of his reckoning. The jinn replied that such was the case. He explained that the vessels had been cast into the sea of El Kerker, along whose shores lived an ancient people whose ancestor was Noah. The great servant of The Lord had alighted there after the deluge, but had become separated from the other sons of Adam.

The sheikh then obtained intelligence from the jinn regarding the path that the party must follow to come to the City of Brass, and thereafter the Sea of El Kerker. Knowing which way they must travel, the group then made haste toward their destination.

After a while, the caravan sighted a wall of black in the distance, at the corners of which were what appeared to be two giant fires raging against each other.

"Praise be to Allah!" cried the sheikh, "We have come at last to the City of Brass! For I have read that it is described as such in the *Book of Hidden Treasures*! Its high walls of dark stone are bounded by two towers of Andalusia brass, which appear to be aflame when viewed from a distance."

The party soon came upon the city, but found that the gate would not open up to them. There were twenty-five portals around the city walls, not yet visible to them. The sheikh recalled that the *Book of Hidden Treasures* told that these gates could only be opened from inside the city.

Talib proposed that they wait awhile, trusting that God might reveal a way by which they may gain entry. They charged one from their number to ride around the city wall on a camel, from which he might observe a means of entry. But after three days, the scout returned from his mission, advising that the easiest point of entry was at the very point where the group had settled.

The emir, Talib and the sheikh then retired to mount a hill that overlooked the city. From here, they could survey the magnificence of the place, and saw that it was silent and deserted, except for the roosts of many birds of the desert. Mousa was filled with sorrow at what he saw. Then, turning to their side, the three men observed seven tablets of fine white marble, beckoning their attention from a distance.

The tablets became clear to them, and they came to see that each bore an inscription. The sheikh read from the first of them:

"How heedless are you of what has gone before you! Do you not know that the cup of death is already filled for you, yet still you cast your eyes aside? Examine yourselves before you descend into your graves. Where now are those who once were held in majesty here, but who abused God's service? Now they have given up the high walls of their palaces for the shallow carriages of their graves! Neither mighty armies nor all the world's riches could ward off their fate!"

As the sheikh finished his reading, the emir cried out, "Surely it is most fitting to abstain from the pleasures of this world!" He took note of what he had heard, as he had written down the warnings that had preceded him, and would again record those that he was yet to hear.

The second tablet then came into view:

"Why are you seduced? Why do you forget that the day is fast approaching when you must settle your debts? Where now are the kings who peopled Irak and ruled over the four quarters of this world? Where are those who held power in Ispahan and in the land of Khorassan? What they built and fortified could save them not!"

After protesting his awe once more, the emir bade the sheikh to read from the third tablet:

"You make yourself busy with your love for the world, and turn your attention away from the commands of your God. Prepare to give answer for the path that you have chosen!"

The emir wept more, then heard what was written on the fourth tablet:

"For how much longer shall your Lord bear with you and your addiction to man's delights? Remember that death awaits you. Hasten to make provision for your fateful encounter!"

As Mousa quaked still further, the sheikh turned to read from the fifth tablet:

"Why are you distracted from obeying your only Creator? You do not acknowledge his bounty, and are ungrateful for his favours. Beware to fare well and take heed of these warnings, lest you perish!"

The sixth tablet then revealed its warning:

"Do not believe that you will be immune for ever. Your forefathers have now all passed into dust. All now pay for what they embraced!"

From the seventh tablet, the sheikh read:

"Know that death is ready for you, bearing heavily upon your shoulders! Prepare for its onset! Trust only in the Lord of Lords! Recognise the instability of this world, which may be likened to a spider's web that draws attention from all who come near it, yet catches all, and demands the lives of all!"

The emir beat his body and was stricken with fear. In his eyes, the treasures of the world now suddenly lost their significance, and he knew well that the warnings that he had heard would surely soon come to pass.

Deeply troubled by their encounter with the tablets, the men descended the hill to rejoin their camp. Still, they questioned how they might enter the city, where they could discover rich pickings that they might take to please their caliph.

At length, Talib proposed that they build a ladder. Carpenters and blacksmiths were called to set about the task. Within one month, they built a tall and sturdy ladder, which was then set against the wall.

One of the men volunteered to ascend the ladder, to see if he might discover a way for entering the city. When he reached the top, he clapped his hands in joy, but was at once crushed by the might of Allah!

Another man then came forward to offer his service, claiming that the first man was a madman, whose insanity had overcome him.

However, when he reached the top of the ladder, this second man also let out a cry of joy, then was dashed to pieces. Presently, a third man came forward from the company to climb the ladder; then a fourth, and a fifth, until fully twelve men had made the ascent, one after the other perishing as they set eyes on what lay beyond the wall.

The emir feared that none could resist a power that would take so many worthy men, and proposed that they should at once leave the city. But finally the sheikh came forward to volunteer to undertake the perilous task himself, claiming that his experience might save him, and that it was his wish to be the bringer of what the party desired.

His companions begged him not to forsake them, for they were fearful for his life and were dependent on his guidance. But the sheikh remained resolute, and started to go slowly up the ladder.

When he stood on the city wall, the sheikh looked down below him, and began to laugh. Then he took strength to meditate on the Glorious Names of God.

At last, he called out to the emir that he need not have fear, as Allah had protected him from the deceit of Satan. Ten maidens had beckoned to him from below, showing him a lake into which he could throw himself from the wall. But the sheikh had resisted their temptation, and so their illusion vanished. He observed that this powerful sorcery was doubtless intended to ensnare anyone who sought entry to the city.

The sheikh then proceeded to walk along the city wall, until he came to one of the towers of brass. Set into the tower was a gigantic gate made of gold, but not having any visible means of opening. Close to where he was standing, the sheikh caught sight of a statue of a horseman, whose outstretched hand held high a banner. On it was written the instruction: "Turn the pin in my navel twelve times, and the gate will open for you!"

The sheikh followed this instruction, and promptly the gate was opened. He then rejoined his party, which decided to make entry into the great city. It was agreed that half of the party should remain outside, lest it not be safe for all to venture within. The others started along a long passageway, where they observed the bodies of many guardsmen, who had fallen silent when life had escaped them.

They then came to a large marketplace, surrounded by imposing buildings. Here too, they found many dead—merchants and beggars alike. The route then led them through a gold souk, a souk where once were sold fine silks, and then to two more, where the finest perfumes and other exotic wares were once traded.

Here too, the townsfolk had fallen lifeless, their canopies and their houses no longer serving them any useful purpose.

The group then came upon a lofty palace, whose towering door beckoned them to enter. The bodies of deceased guardsmen greeted them, and they saw still more as they ventured in, seeing the swords of the guards that were still ready to be drawn, and encountering other long-gone servants, resting on benches of precious ivory.

The sheikh read from an inscription that was set into one of the walls:

"Consider well what your eyes behold here, O mortals! Take heed of the fate of those who preceded you, being the same ending that you will surely endure! Observe here those who set their love on opulent luxuries, but whose artefacts protected them not. What they adored gives them no pleasure now. In their slumber, all hope for them is gone."

Seeing what these men had lost, and what they could never regain, the emir couldn't prevent his tears from flowing once more.

The travellers then went further into the inner palace, where they came upon a vast atrium, which was overlooked by a large pavilion in each of its four corners. At the centre was a fountain, sprouting from an ornate column that rested upon a plinth of moonstone and melanite.

The first pavilion that the men visited was filled with gold and rubies, the second with gleaming armoury. In the third–behind curtains of scarlet and purple–they found many weapons, each inlaid with precious stones. The fourth contained closets filled with plates, goblets, crystals, and other vessels for eating and drinking.

Each man took from what he found according to his wishes. The party then moved further toward the heart of the palace, proceeding beyond a silk curtain, whose opening the sheikh was able to discern.

There, they saw elaborate tapestries lining the walls of a corridor that led them forward. Beyond this, they encountered a saloon, which hosted a grand pavilion, which itself was crowned with a dome of great majesty.

The dome towered over a canopy, on which were embroidered figures of many beasts of the sky. Beneath this stood a couch on a raised platform on which lay a damsel. The damsel appeared to be alive, for her eyes shone like silver. Two immobile slaves stood in front of the couch, protecting the marble steps that led up to the platform.

On one of the steps was an inscription, which the sheikh translated for the benefit of his companions:

"How ignorant you are in your unceasing hope; how heedless of the warnings of your unavoidable end! Prepare for your grave, for time will not attend you for much longer!

"Know that I am Tedmureh, daughter of the kings of the Amalekites, who once held dominion here. I possess that which no other possessed, being right and just. For many years I lived, until calamity overtook our land. Through seven years of drought we suffered, until there was nothing remaining for us to eat. The Treasury could not buy food from abroad, and so we resigned ourselves to the Will of God and shut firm the gates of our city, awaiting our fate.

"Fear of Allah is the only surety! Be not seduced away from serving your Lord. I whom you see wasn't so deluded, making provision for my appointed day. Who visits here may take what they will, but not from anything that lies on my body. These are to furnish me for my final journey. Fear God, lest He destroys you!"

Deeply troubled by this dire warning, the emir instructed his company to fetch and load their camels. At last, he heeded the princess's command, commanding his men that nothing should be taken from her body.

Talib questioned his wisdom, mocking the words that all had heard. "Surely these goods are worth more to us than the damsel who now lies sleeping?" he protested. Without having regard for the emir's instruction, he mounted the steps toward the couch, in order to take from there what his heart desired.

No sooner had he made clear his intention, than one of the slaves suddenly became animated, and cut off his head.

The remainder of the company then left the city, securing its mighty gate behind them. They then made haste for the seashore, as the Afreet imprisoned in the column had advised them, journeying for one month more.

After a time they encountered tall mountains, below which they observed many natives, who made their dwellings in caves.

At first, the party feared that they had stumbled upon a city of jinn. But the sheikh was emboldened to seek audience with their king, who proclaimed that they were men, and descendants of Noah besides. The sea that washed up on the shore was the Sea of El

Kerker, and all the natives swore allegiance to Allah, and honoured the precious name of His prophet, Mohammed (peace be upon him).

The emir explained the purpose of their expedition to the king, saying that they were servants of the great caliph, who sought possession of one or more copper vessels that he had been told the Lord Solomon had once cast into the sea that was close to here.

The party's hosts promised to assist the travellers in achieving their quest, begging them to accept their hospitality while they sent divers to fetch some twelve of the desired vessels from the sea's bed.

The emir gave thanks for the natives' generosity, and offered them gifts in return. Thereupon, the caravan departed on its long journey to Damascus, making quickly to present their cargo to the caliph.

When they arrived, they told the caliph all that had happened, and described the grave manner by which Talib had met his end.

Then the caliph opened each vessel in turn, from which devils came forth—one after another—each howling their repentance.

The caliph was full of wonder at what he saw. "Never did Allah give a man the likes of that which He bestowed upon Solomon the Wise!" he exclaimed.

The spoils of the mission were distributed amongst the faithful. Mousa sought the caliph's favour to appoint his son governor of North Africa in his stead, such that he might journey to Jerusalem, where he might offer worship to his God. This is where he died.

This is the story that has come down to us about the City of Brass. Heed its message well! May God The All-Knowing be praised!

Via Frances

Todd and I have been friends since first grade. He was my first and only boyfriend, and it never seemed in doubt that we would one day marry. We attended the same Bible class during our teens, and then went through college together. Only when Todd entered the Southern Baptist Theological Seminary in Louisville to train for ministry did we live in different cities, but even then, he used to visit me every weekend.

We married soon after Todd was ordained, and moved to west Lexington, where he took up a post as an associate pastor. Todd has always been jealous for his faith. At times, his passion has threatened to get the better of him–igniting his fiery temper, and causing him to disbelieve that another person's opinion might hold any weight. His years of study have made him a walking concordance of the Bible, and he is able to quote any verse at whim. He is especially sharp at referencing chapter and verse whenever he needs to confront any challenge that is put to him.

My style is less aggressive, but I love my Lord Jesus no less passionately than Todd. "Karen, you are the perfect wife for our boy," Todd's parents have often told me. "You know how to keep him in check, and make a good home for him."

It's true that I do feel content in my role as a home-loving wife, baking and cooking for him, and making sure that his pants and shirts are always neatly pressed. Since he became our church's pastor, I've felt all the more proud to support him in his busy and important work.

You might say that ours is a marriage that was truly made in heaven. Good friends we have been for many years, and I can't deny that Todd has always been the only one for me. But that's not to say that our partnership hasn't passed over some rocky ground.

The main problem has been Todd's inability to control his insatiable sex drive. His small minister's stipend has often been spent on prostitutes and glossy mags, while I often suspected that Todd wasn't always being fully truthful to me when he made excuses for his occasional absences.

In the main, we managed to ride through our difficulties. Todd at least acknowledged that he had a problem, and opened up to a few of the deacons, who were able to offer him some man-to-man counselling.

Recently, Todd had become better able to confine himself to the house, but he was still spending half the night glued to his computer screen. He used to tell me that he was working on his sermons, or dealing with pastoral matters, but I know what kind of work was really preoccupying him.

Of course, we'd talked about his addiction many times, trying to square his behaviour with the teachings of our Lord. Todd often showed great remorse, crying disconsolately when confessing his sins. Each time, he promised to put right his wayward ways, but it was never long before he was back in front of the computer screen again.

Encouraged by the deacons, for a while Todd joined with a group of men who shared his obsession. The therapist who led the group was a member of our church, but he acted discreetly, showing great love and compassion for Todd—as should a true brother in Christ.

Todd committed to the course of therapy and managed to avoid his nightly Internet surfing for a while, but after a couple of months, he again succumbed to temptation and went back to his old ways.

We might have gone on like this for many years had a shameful incident not interrupted us in a way that was to change our lives. Todd had left me at home for a weekend while he attended a Southern Baptist Convention meeting in Louisville. At least, that's where he told me he was going.

He did not return the following week when I expected him to. Following a night of worrying, and having been unable to reach him on his cell phone, I contacted the State Police to report him missing. They made some enquiries, and quickly established that he was being held in custody by the Louisville Metro Police Department.

Todd had been arrested for accosting a prostitute, whom he'd picked up while cruising the streets in his Chevy. The pair had disagreed over the price that had been arranged for the girl's services, and erupting into a serious rage, Todd had threatened to hit the woman. This was when she decided to call the police. Apparently, both had been drinking.

I felt sickened when I heard the news. However, I knew that it was my responsibility to support my husband. I left quickly for Louisville, where I met the attorney who had been appointed to represent Todd. He told me that charges were unlikely to be brought, because Todd hadn't actually carried through his threat, while the testimony that had been given by the drunken woman was unlikely to be considered sufficiently strong evidence to secure a conviction. I felt relieved to hear this news, but hadn't anticipated the aftermath that was to follow.

A journalist had picked up on the news of Todd's arrest, and by some means had been able to identify him as a Baptist pastor. Soon, the news of my husband's escapade with the prostitute had made not only the front page of the *Louisville Courier-Journal*, but had carried across the state to Lexington too. I dreaded to think what the decent people of our church would say when they saw the photograph of their pastor being paraded in front of a police identification plate.

When we returned to Lexington, most people seemed to want to avoid mentioning the topic. It was obvious to me that they had been deeply unsettled by Todd's indiscretion. To our faces at least, they promised their love, assuring us that ours is a God of love, able to forgive every sinner—even a wayward minister.

Todd was not afraid to show his contrition before his flock. Were Oscars awarded for emotional outpouring by those in church ministry, Todd would surely be nominated for an award. Whether or not his tears were genuine I do not know, but he certainly gave a powerful example of how to show repentance when he took his place on the dais.

"O my Father, how I have failed you! How I have let these, my beloved brothers and sisters, down! Forgive me, for I am the worse among sinners!"

His cries and wailing knew no limit. Kneeling before the congregation, Todd accepted the prayers and blessings of the people. Two of the deacons laid hands on him, commanding the demons that were in him to depart.

Perhaps this display was good for our community. Other men in the congregation came forward to confess their infidelity, and to receive the forgiveness of the Lord Jesus and those of us who serve Him. In fact, I don't think that our church had for a long time felt so overcome by the love and warmth of The Holy Spirit.

The experience had certainly been a shock for Todd. He knew that his position as a pastor would be under threat were he to backslide again. More than anything, I think that he was genuinely aware that he'd been unfaithful to his Lord.

He had been unfaithful to me too, and privately I went through a period of hurt and suffering. But the fast pace of events, and Todd's apparent regret for his actions, kept me focused on supporting my husband.

When the excitement that had taken hold of our church settled down, Todd accepted one of his deacon friend's offer to counsel him, and to share in one-to-one prayer. I think that this man's company was good for Todd, and especially since he was recognised as a wise elder in our community.

I wasn't of course privy to their discussions, but it soon became clear that Todd was considering taking a sabbatical, leaving care for the church in the hands of the deacons and our associate pastor. His friend had suggested that Todd might like to take a trip to Europe, possibly to travel along one of the old pilgrim routes to the holy city of Santiago de Compostela.

We'd heard about the popularity of the Camino paths, though not being Roman Catholics, we'd not considered the possibility of undertaking such a journey ourselves. Intrigued by the deacon's earnest suggestion, Todd began to read about the experiences of other travellers. I too soon found myself reading of the adventures of Shirley MacLaine, Paulo Coelho, and their like.

Certain that our own pilgrimage would be good for our spiritual development, as well as for strengthening the bonds of our marriage, we committed ourselves to follow in the footsteps of the many who'd journeyed to Spain before us. We made arrangements to hand over our responsibilities for the church, and then began to plan our expedition to the place where the remains of St. James were finally laid to rest.

Our deacon friend had a contact in southern France, whom he felt certain would be happy to host us following our arrival in Europe. He was a Jesuit priest, who apparently made a habit of welcoming pilgrims of any denomination.

Our flight to Paris was my first overseas. After a brief but magical day admiring the sights of the French capital, we took a train south to Biarritz, where we were met by Father Xavier. Since we spoke virtually no French, we were grateful that this kindly man's English was of a standard that few back home achieve by their eleventh grade. A short but stout man, Father Xavier had retired from full-time ministry several years before, and now spent much of his time hosting pilgrims before they set off on the Camino.

We were grateful for the good Father's advice about what we might expect to find along our way, and appreciated the chance to relax for a couple of days in his simple but peaceful lodgings.

During the last day of our stay with him, Father Xavier asked us what we hoped to achieve from completing our walk. He graciously listened to us, gently challenging us to go deeper to find our purpose.

I imagine that this is what he saw as being one of his primary roles–to help travellers set off in a true spirit of pilgrimage, rather than seeing the Camino as an exercise in completing one of a traveller's "must do's".

Todd's pilgrimage was about connecting more deeply with the Lord. He was certain that if he constantly had Jesus in his life, he would never be able to stray. My main purpose was to deepen my love for God, and through this, to become a better wife for Todd.

When we bade our goodbye to Father Xavier, we made for the town of St Jean Pied de Port–a beautiful, bustling place, that's traditionally regarded as one of the starting points for the Camino Frances, the best known of the pilgrim's routes to Santiago. Bearing our heavy rucksacks, with our sleeping pouches and water bottles attached, we set off from St Jean Pied de Port toward the tiny village of Roncesvalles, where we planned to make our first night's stay.

Father Xavier had warned us that our first day of walking would not be easy. We admitted that we were not practiced walkers, rarely venturing far outside of Lexington, and then normally only driving one hundred miles or so to catch a ballgame. I'd enjoyed horseback riding when I was younger, but now I was far from being in top physical condition.

Our passage through the high Roncesvalles Pass across the Pyrenees took a full twelve hours. Whenever we approached the top of a slope where we were certain that the path would level out, another high ridge came into view. We took regular stops for water, but knew that we had to keep going to avoid what could be trekking in dangerous conditions after dark. Having arrived in Europe in early April, the sun was not yet at its hottest, while a gentle breeze provided us with welcome refreshment as we continued our ascent.

Displaying a calmness that I'd noticed since we arrived in Europe, Todd did little more as we climbed than to admire the beauty of the landscapes we were passing through, as well as occasionally sharing conversation with some of the *perigrinos* that we passed, who were making the same journey.

Many of our fellow travellers explained their reasons for making the pilgrimage. Most spoke about their desire to deepen their own understanding of themselves, as did we. Knowing that we might not meet many of them again after our expedition ended, Todd felt free to talk about his profession and his misdemeanours. Whenever he related his story, Todd declared his gratefulness to the Lord and expressed regret for having ever transgressed.

Finally we came to the small village of Roncesvalles, where we were grateful to find space in a comfortable *refugio*. Here, we collected the first of a collection of hostel stamps in our *credencial*—a sort of passport carried by pilgrims. We would need a decent collection of stamps to show when we finally reached Santiago, in order to be awarded with our *compostela* certificate, confirming the completion of our great journey.

The accommodation was basic, but we were happy to do no more than fill our bellies with a hearty bowl of soup, then settle into our dormitories. Our first and possibly most strenuous day over, Todd and I quickly found ourselves drifting into a peaceful sleep.

The second day of our pilgrimage involved many hours of climbing and then descending, as we made our way across a couple of passes. We then came upon the first of two villages where we had the option to spend the night. While weary and eager for our supper, we decided to carry on to the furthest of the two, since this would give us extra time to spare when we arrived at Pamplona, which we were due to set sight upon the following day.

Our longer walk proved to be a good idea, since we took only a few hours to reach Pamplona the next morning. Todd was keen to see the ancient church of San Nicolás, which we heard dated from the 12th century. We also took time to see the imposing Gothic Cathedral, with its breathtaking cloister and dramatic facade. While I loved the bluegrass and endless weatherboard buildings of my homeland, we had nothing to compare with this in Kentucky.

Todd was keen to enquire about the famous bull running that takes place in the city every year. I think that he was disappointed that we hadn't timed our visit to coincide with the colourful festival. Seeing the stampede of red-blooded men charging through the city would have appealed to his appetite for rough sports and macho bravado.

Our stay in Pamplona was as comfortable as our two previous nights, but we were beginning to feel the consequences of our eagerness to reach there. Skin was beginning to bubble on the soles of our feet, and already a couple of fully formed blisters were adding pain to every step.

We were able to shop in Pamplona for a couple of provisions that we'd forgotten to pack. Todd was pleased to finally have shower gel of his own, having had to borrow from others the two previous nights.

The fourth stage of our journey involved further climbing, this time taking in the Alto del Perdon, or "Hill of Forgiveness". We didn't discover how the hill earned its name, but the glorious rainbow that unfolded behind the tree line on the summit was–Todd was certain–a message that God had well and truly forgiven him.

When we reached the top of the hill, we stopped to admire a statue honouring earlier pilgrims, and then made a careful descent down the difficult slopes toward our next place of rest.

Along our way, we noticed a reference to Scripture, a verse that someone had chalked on a large rock at one side of the path: "Do not be amazed at this, for a time is coming when all who are in their graves will hear His voice and come out—those who have done what is good will rise to live, and those who have done what is evil will rise to be condemned."

Todd recognized the text as being from the Gospel of John (of course, being able to quote chapter and verse). He took the admonition as a portent for him to remain on the steady course. While saying nothing more, I could see that he was greatly troubled by finding this written here.

Most of the Camino was well signposted. We knew that we were still on the right path whenever we came across a sign bearing an image of a scallop shell, the symbol of the Camino. As we came down the Hill of Forgiveness, we realised that we hadn't noticed a route marker for some time.

"Do you figure we might be lost?" I enquired, becoming increasingly worried that we wouldn't reach our next planned destination before dark.

"Give me the map!" Todd snapped, certain that he'd be able to pinpoint our current location.

"I see where we are!" he asserted, pointing at the map to show me where I should have been looking. "I should have known better than to let you be in charge of the map!" he complained. "Women just aren't good at figuring out directions."

I let his comment pass, as I'd ignored so many of his sexist swipes before. Todd justified his pig-headedness by pointing to what the apostle Paul told the Corinthians in his first epistle to the church there: "Christ is the head of every man, and the man is the head of a woman, and God is the head of Christ." It wasn't helpful for me to mention the teaching in Genesis that God had created man and woman equally–Todd had always been quick to remind me that it was Eve rather than Adam who was first tempted to eat the apple.

We continued our descent of the hill, stopping at a point that we supposed was about half an hour's walk from the village we were aiming for. Here, we were able to admire a magnificent sunset. A peregrine falcon soared overhead, circling repeatedly as it searched for prey. The fresh fragrance of the pine trees that lined our path added to the preciousness of the moment.

Ahead of us, we saw what looked like the perimeter wall of a monastery, its grey-black silhouette contrasting starkly against the reddening sky. Two tall towers appeared to stand at either end of the building, casting an impressive sight.

We felt certain that the *refugio* that we hoped to make our next resting place lay just beyond the sight line of the monastery, even though the structure didn't appear to be marked on our map.

We made good speed toward the imposing edifice, discovering when we arrived that it was in fact a ruin, and that there was no sign of a village beyond. With dusk intensifying its grip, we set down our backpacks, conceding that we were lost.

"What the heck are we going to do?" yelled Todd, reprimanding me as though it were my fault that we found ourselves in the predicament we were in. "Where the hell are we going to sleep?"

My immediate concern was to relieve the pressure on my agonising feet, which I felt would be incapable of carrying me any further. Several large blisters were now fully formed.

"There's nothing for it, honey, but to set up camp here for the night," I replied.

"But there's no fucking toilet here, you stupid woman!" he hollered, "No fucking roof, no fucking shower, no fucking place to eat!"

Todd only swore when he was really angry, an occasion that always involved finding someone to blame. I felt very uncomfortable when he reacted this way, knowing that in a moment of poor control, he had the ability to lash out.

"I'm sorry, honey," I stammered. "You're probably right, it is my fault that we've ended up in this mess. But we have a couple of Snickers bars in your bag, and our sleeping bags are surely good enough to keep us warm?"

My attempt to appease Todd calmed him a little, and after continued ranting and rough rummaging through his bag, he acknowledged that we had little option than to bed down for the night where we were.

I stroked his head and gently caressed him, doing my best to comfort and reassure him. I tried to make him see that God had allowed us to come to this place for a reason. Everything that had happened on our journey so far was guided by His hand.

"The angels are with us, honey," I promised him. "Just like they were for the shepherds on that hill when the baby Jesus was born. Who knows, we might get to see a bright star ourselves tonight when the full play of the night puts on its show?"

We each took time digesting our Snickers bars, giving out tongues much longer than usual to explore their rich mix of flavours and textures. Then–fully clothed–we slipped into our sleeping bags, and lay back to admire the brilliant night sky.

"The heavens declare the glory of God, the sky displays His handiwork," whispered Todd, quoting a verse from one of the Psalms. "You're right to remind me that we've got a lot to be grateful for. Look at those stars! Have you ever seen a sky as beautiful as that?"

Todd lent over to kiss me, then rested his head against the hood of his sleeping bag, and quickly fell asleep. I took longer to follow him, still marvelling at the brilliance of the light show in the heavens. I'd read that in earlier times, pilgrims had used the Milky Way to navigate their route along the Camino. Perhaps the likes of earlier *perigrinos* like Chaucer, Charlemagne, and El Cid had seen the very sky that was so absorbing my attention now?

I felt at peace, and soon forgot about the relentless burning that my feet wanted me to attend to. After reflecting on the day's adventure for sometime, I eventually succumbed to my tiredness and joined Todd in a chorus of snoring.

I slept for what must have been many hours, because when I awoke, the sun had already risen close to its maximum height. I turned to see if Todd was still sleeping, but his sleeping bag was already packed away. I pulled myself out of my own sack, and started to look around for Todd.

"Todd! Todd! Where are you?" I cried. Todd didn't reply. I clambered over the half-walls of the ruin, still calling out for my husband. I tried calling his cell phone, but got no reply. After a time it dawned on me— Todd had gone on without me.

I found myself panting and shaking, unable to keep my calm. Where on earth had he gone? I desperately asked myself. What had I done to cause him to go off without a word?

I could fathom no answer, believing that the argument that we'd had the previous day had been buried by the time we fell asleep. But I knew that Todd had an impetuous nature, and was prone to storming off in a sulk whenever he felt that he'd been undermined.

I was very shaken, and unsure why Todd hadn't wanted to talk to me first. Had he left in a mad moment of stupidity, much like a schizophrenic temporary takes leave of their senses? Did he mean to end our marriage? And what on earth had prompted him to undo all of the good work that he'd achieved during the past couple of months to overcome his addiction?

I searched around the area for some time, but decided at last that I must attempt to find my way back onto the Camino, hoping that I would be able to catch up with Todd at the next *refugio*.

Slowly, and in great pain, I retraced my steps up the Hill of Forgiveness, then came upon a scallop sign, that set me back on the well-trodden path to the town of Puente La Reina.

I arrived early at the *refugio*, beating the usual queues of over-nighters, who had at times threatened to claim all the beds that the hostel could offer even before we arrived.

Todd hadn't checked in at the *refugio*. I felt certain that he would not have carried on to the next resting place, which his suffering feet would surely not be capable of carrying him to in a single day. Conscious of my own pain, I decided that I had no option than to spend the night where I was, then to continue the search for my husband the following morning. I reasoned that I might be able to enlist the help of other *perigrinos* to make enquiries about his whereabouts.

I didn't have to wait long before discovering where Todd had gone to. My next day's walk brought me to Estella-Lizarra, a charming town that catered well for the needs of pilgrims. I enquired about Todd at various *refugios*, to see if any had provided accommodation for him the previous night. The warden at one told me that Todd had passed through, and she thought that he then planned to check into a local hotel. He had wanted to stay another night at the hostel, but they'd told him that he would have to find another place to stay after he had returned drunk the night before. He was lucky to have been allowed back into the *refugio* that night.

I then made enquiries at several of the town's hotels, finally discovering the one that Todd had chosen as his resting place for the night. I checked into the same place, then waited in the lounge until I caught sight of him.

It was now late evening, and Todd did not notice me at first, possibly because he had been drinking. Without looking around, he made his way across the lounge to a computer terminal that had been set up in one corner, allowing guests to connect to the Internet. It was obvious what sort of search results he was keen for Google to bring up.

I waited for a while before making my move. I stood behind Todd, unsurprised to see that he was back to his old habit of hunting down online porn.

I continued watching him for some moments, while Todd remained unaware of my presence. Then I slapped him around the head and shouted, "What the hell do you think you're doing? Haven't you given me enough to worry about by taking off without me?

What the hell is the point of making this damn trip if you don't make the slightest effort to crack your habit?"

After my outburst, I went back to my seat across the room. Todd logged off the computer, then came across to where I was sitting. Without a hint of regret, he snapped, "No one tells me where I can go and what I can do! When are you going to learn that, you stupid woman? I've seen enough of you already today. I'm going out!"

Stunned by his tantrum, I burst into tears. Todd was unaffected by my weeping, and stormed out of the room, as he'd threatened.

I don't know where he went that night, but he didn't check out of the hotel until the following morning. By then, his mood had changed considerably, and we were able to sit down over breakfast and have a long conversation.

⅋⁀

Todd was much less agitated than I'd often seen him, seeming to be very thoughtful and taken in by something. He was obviously very tired.

He began by showering me with compliments, and repeatedly apologised for his behaviour the previous few days.

"Something's really got stirred up for me during this walk," he started. "I know that Father Xavier warned us that a lot of inner stuff comes up when you take the Camino seriously, but I had no idea just how much I was carrying."

While I was very angry at Todd's actions–which seemed to me to be totally selfishly driven–I accepted that he hadn't acted in a normal state of mind.

"I promise you, honey, I didn't go where you thought I might go last night," he went on. "There was no more web surfing, no more alcohol. I just started wandering around the town, feeling depressed and confused, unsure what was happening in my life.

"I might even have been talking aloud to myself, or letting my tears show–I don't know how others saw me, I was in such a state. A man had apparently been following me for sometime, keeping an eye on me from the other side of the street, where he was walking his dog. After a while, he approached me, and, perhaps because I had been letting out occasional cries, he asked me in broken English whether I was all right.

"I obviously wasn't, because his question prompted me to break into a full-blown cry. The man did his best to reassure me, then led me to his house, where he invited me to tell him what was troubling me.

"We spoke for what I suppose were many hours, working our way through two full cafetieres of coffee. The man listened very carefully, gently consoling me. It turned out that he too had once suffered from a terrible temper, which had eventually been the ruin of his marriage. He had since become something of a recluse, though he gave his time to a support group, which aimed to help men work through their problems.

"The man was at pains to warn me about the course on which I was headed. He challenged me to consider how much I valued my friendship with you, and to see what a rock you have been to me through all of our years together. I felt very sad and ashamed when I reflected on the appalling way that I've often treated you.

"This gracious man also questioned me about the strength of my faith. We read from the Bible together, and I felt more shame than I have ever done for constantly failing both you and my Lord.

"When the man brought me back to the hotel, I sat on my bed, grieving over the pain that I've caused you. My heart pounding and my cheeks wet from my tears, I promised Jesus that I would never let you down again, nor fail in my service to him.

"This is when I felt the most magnificent peace. My whole body filled with the warm assurance of the Holy Spirit—I knew that God had sent His Counsellor to help me! My tears of regret turned to tears of joy, as the Spirit took hold of my whole being!"

Todd paused at this point. I leant over the small table to where we had been seated for breakfast to kiss him, gently resting my hands on his arms.

"We're on this journey together, Todd," I promised. "Come what may, I'm not going to let you go astray."

We finished our meal in silence, then decided to extend our stay in Estella for a few days more.

When we felt ready, we began again on the Camino. The first stage after our rest involved a long day's walking, but took us through some spectacular wine country. It was here that the famous Rioja is produced.

Todd and I walked hand-in-hand for most of the way, content and grateful for the beautiful world that we were able to explore together.

We continued along the Camino for another couple of weeks, sharing stories with passing *perigrinos*, and taking stock of all of the blessings that we'd received.

By the time we reached León, we decided that we had no need to continue our pilgrimage. Neither of us cared for the accolade of reaching Santiago Cathedral, nor were we concerned about whether or not we collected our *compostela* certificates. As Father Xavier had told us, true pilgrims make the Camino journey in their hearts–and these are journeys that have no end.

We spent our last night in a *refugio*, then took a coach back to San Sebastián, close to the border with France. From there, we travelled on to Biarritz, where we related our story and repeated our thanks to Father Xavier.

We have been back in Kentucky for six months
now, although it seems like barely a few days since we
were roaming in the mountains. The church organised
a wonderful party to welcome us back, and of course
everyone wanted to know about our experiences.

Todd has taken on a less aggressive style with his
preaching, though with no less conviction about what
he believes. To date, he's not ventured near a bar, nor
spent any of his evenings in front of his computer. I
feel that he accepts me more as an equal partner now,
and I'm sticking to my promise to stay with him—
whatever lies ahead for us, wherever we might wander.
Praise the Lord for His goodness to us!

Afterword

The story of the *City of Brass* contains many motifs
and metaphors, marking it out as one of the most complex to interpret among the tales from the *Nights*.
This is complicated by the fact that there are different
versions of the story. Commentators aren't agreed on
how the symbolism in the tale should be interpreted.

The original translation of this text contains much
religious allegory, especially in describing the eloquent
inscriptions that the men encounter. Both for the sake
of brevity, and because I am not able to offer a translation from the Arabic, I have chosen to heavily summa-
rise much of the religious references in my retelling of

the original tale. While this may reduce the significance of this aspect, I believe that it shouldn't affect the plotline and essential messages of the story.

The story tells of a long journey into the unknown, which the party embarks upon to satisfy a curiosity about the actions of Solomon, the legend of which has come down to them through oral tradition.

With the sheikh able to offer partial guidance and act as an interpreter of the various inscriptions that the travellers encounter, it is Talib's knowledge of the *Book of Hidden Treasures*, and the caliph's desire to witness the breaking open of one of Solomon's vessels for himself, that motivates this perilous adventure.

The party is driven off course when they're unable to rely on familiar means for navigation. Then, it becomes necessary for them to act on their feelings to find their way forward. Fortune smiles on them at several points, and they are given direction to help them take the next step along their way. When they remain faithful to the guidance they are given, they are ultimately able to follow the path that leads them back to a familiar road.

However, the group is easily distracted. Tempted by the allure, first of the black castle, and then of the City of Brass, they cannot but help themselves from venturing further and further in the hope of uncovering more marvels and treasures.

This might not be unlike the drive of many expeditions that have come across the legacies of past civilizations. And, like more recent adventurers, the party feels it is its right to plunder treasure from the places they encounter, justifying their actions by claiming that the citizens who had once possessed them now have no further need for worldly goods. They do not appreciate that everything has its place, nor give full respect to the spirits of those who have passed on.

The castle and the City of Brass do not give up their secrets easily. So grand and marvellous are they, that the emir and his companions go to great lengths to discover ways of penetrating them. Even the very towers of the great city appear to be smoke in the mirage that first greets the travellers; almost imitating the spirits that have departed from the place, and yet which still twist and swirl about.

The fate of the deceased make clear their warnings. Were they further to doubt their truth, the taking of Talib's life presents the emir and his company with the clearest example of the message. The party comes to ultimate faith through experience; the caliph's faith too is rewarded by his witnessing the repenting of the jinn when they are unlocked from their copper prisons, vividly proving a legacy of Solomon's.

The maidens who entice the soldiers who climb the city walls are allusions too, appealing to the carnal urges of man. Only the sheikh is wise enough to recognise their deception, and to stand firm against the temptation that is set before him.

The warnings to avoid being deluded by worldly riches come one after the other. Yet time after time, the party is impelled to press on with its mission to explore further, perhaps hopeful of encountering more treasure. This they do when they loot from the coffers in the palace's pavilions.

Each time he is reminded of his mortality, the emir proclaims his trust in The Almighty. Perhaps too, each time he grieves over the struggle that he faces in giving up on worldly delights, like the many who struggled before him.

The castle and the city enrapture the explorers as might a dream. And, as in a dream, they are led deeper and deeper in a test of their base motives.

The setting, of course, is a desert, where the illusions of a mirage commonly but deceitfully beckon weary travellers to find rest and nourishment. It's perhaps then no surprise that one commentator has described this as being the "gloomiest of travelogues"[3].

It takes the words of the righteous princess to finally shake the emir from his struggle. Among the party, only Talib—the one called 'Seeker of Treasures'—

---

[3] Hamori, A, in Marzolph, U (2006) *Arabian Nights Reader*, Wayne State University Press, p 283.

remains undaunted by this final warning. He is the one that will never turn around his heart, and the destruction that this guarantees comes quickly upon him.

The journey home appears to be much less fraught than the outbound one. Their mission accomplished, and now not giving in to the temptation to stray, the party makes a steady path to Damascus, eager to bring pleasure to their caliph.

The reclining princess, whilst dead, is mistaken for being alive. This may be a reference to a story in Islamic literature of a prince who, when straying from his palace during his wedding feast, mistakes a corpse that he finds in a cemetery for his bride. Hamori remarks on this possible reference, suggesting that it may have been intended as "a gnostic parable of the soul's pre-existence and return from its terrestrial sojourn"[1].

The full might of Solomon's power is clearly described in the story. Here is a man that, while human, was given dominion over every living thing, and whose victory over every force that might come against him was assured.

The battle that rages between those who will follow a false idol and those who are faithful to the God of Abraham reaches a climax that should never be in doubt. Still, this is a mother of all battles, raging over

---

[1] Hamori (2006), *op. cit.*, p 293.

a vast territory, and summoning the full might of the powers of the sky.

From his carpet, Solomon has full oversight of his armies and the devils that oppose him. Supported by the hosts–powerful and invisible forces of a heavenly domain–his advantage over his adversary is assured.

Solomon is portrayed as magnificent and invincible. However, one reading of the jinni that is found imprisoned in the column alludes to a story when the king was once said to have lost his ring that gave him his powers[5].

Because of his negligence, power was given in his stead to a jinni for forty days, who impersonated the great king, while Solomon himself took on the guise of an unrecognisable beggar. The jinni that cries out from the column may be an allusion to this one-time pretender.

There is a contrast between the means by which the inhabitants ruled by the king of the sea attempt to protect themselves and the command over natural and godly forces that are bestowed upon Solomon. The former rely on armour and tools that are man-made (brass itself being crafted by human ingenuity); the latter has come to know, and moves with, the power of The Almighty.

---

[5] This is one way in which *Qur'an* 38:34 has been interpreted. See Hamori, *ibid.*, p 283.

As Warner points out[6], Solomon travels through the air, where he has a complete picture of what has happened, is happening, and goes before him below—a big picture that, in a sense, defies the familiar rules of time and space.

With its description of the lengthy distraction that preoccupies the party, and their ultimate coming back to the intended purpose of their expedition, the story tells both of what arises from fortune, and what is predetermined.

Marzolph and van Leeuwen explain in their *Encyclopaedia of the Nights*[7] that the black castle is thought to be situated in lands once ruled over by Alexander the Great. They postulate that the distant cities that the men journey to, far to the west of the caliph's empire, may have been viewed in Islamic literature as being markers of the limits of the world.

Here, perhaps unsurprisingly, the men are faced with visions, words, and appearances that seem to link them with an otherworldly domain. This is the very threshold where the living and the dead are brought face-to-face.

---

[6] Warner, M (2012), *Stranger Magic: Charmed States and the Arabian Nights*, Vintage, p 61.

[7] Marzolph, U and van Leeuwen, R (2004), *The Arabian Nights: An Encyclopaedia*, ABC-CLIO, p 146.

The story makes clear that the provisions any traveller through life should set aside are ones that will nourish the soul, not just include food and drink for the journey[8].

---

[8] Such warning is repeatedly given in Scripture, for example in The *Qur'an* 2:197.

The pilgrim and the old woman who dwelt in the desert

A traveller man once ventured across the desert with a group of fellow pilgrims. This man fell into a deep sleep, and when he awoke, found that his caravan had gone. Not knowing which way he should go, he walked for many miles, before coming upon a tent, in which slept an old woman and her dog.

The pilgrim saluted the woman, and having explained his situation, asked whether she might offer him nourishment to satisfy his hunger.

The woman instructed him, "Go to the valley which you see before you, and there you will find many serpents. Catch some of these, that I might broil them for you."

The man protested that he had never captured serpents before, and that he was afraid to do so. Neither had he eaten them, as they seemed disagreeable to him.

"I shall come with you," offered the woman, "And I will catch some serpents, and then broil them for you."

This the woman did. Seeing that there was no alternative but to eat from what she had brought for him, the man ate the serpent meat.

He then enquired where he might obtain water to quench his burning thirst.

"Go to the well and fetch water from there," replied the woman.

Duly, the man went to the well, but he found the water that he drew from it to be very bitter to his taste. However, with no other means to satisfy his thirst, he drank from it.

The man marvelled at the woman's ability to live in such conditions. "How hard it must be for you to live in this manner," he remarked to her.

"Then tell me how it is in your country?" the woman enquired.

"In the city where I dwell there are many broad boulevards, which are lined with towering trees. Where the boulevards cross are marble-paved squares, each having a lively fountain at its centre," the pilgrim explained. "Rich meats and viands are sold in the marketplace, along with luscious fruit and delightful fish from the oceans. We drink pure water, and dwell in villas that are built of stone."

"This is what I have heard," replied the woman. "But is it not also true that you are ruled by a tyrannical sultan? I am told that if you displease him, or act against his command, he will take away your goods and leave you homeless. You pay for your luxury foods and frivolous life with the corrupt poison of tyranny, but here there is safety and freedom–a healthy recipe. I wager that it is better to be free from tyranny, eating and drinking what the desert provides, and living off her generosity. Do you not know that next to having the true faith, safety and health are the greatest of all Allah's bounties?"

I, who narrate this story, perceive that what the old woman observed is the just rule of the sultan, who is God's vicar on earth. In previous times, it was not necessary for the sultan to rule so viciously, because the people need only see him to fear him. But this is a wicked and depraved generation, and one for which a sultan must be accorded the utmost respect. Were a weak sultan set over this people, calamity would surely come upon the land.

As the proverb declares, "One hundred years of the sultan's tyranny, rather than just one year of the tyranny of the people, who fight one over another." When people turn to fighting among themselves, God appoints a despot to rule over them.

It is said that in days past, Al-Hajjaj ibn Yusuf[9] once received a letter, in which was written, "Fear God and do not oppress his servants."

Heeding these words, Al-Hajjaj took to the pulpit to warn the people of the consequences of their evil deeds. He told them, "Though I will die, your wicked deeds will not deliver you from oppression. If it is not I, then one more greedy for power and cruel in his judgement will rule over you. As it is said, 'There is no hand but that the hand of God is over it, and no oppressor can be worse than He oppresses'. Tyranny is feared, but justice is preferable. We beg Allah to improve our lot."

---

[9] A governor of the Umayyad Caliphate, who ruled in what is now Iraq during the seventh and early eight centuries. Al-Hajjaj was known as a highly capable but harsh leader.

Tissardmine

I've lived in Morocco for five years now, the past three of which I've spent in Tissardmine. This small village lies in the east of the kingdom, and is sited beside an oasis of the Sahara. This is an area not unfamiliar to overland travellers, who seek adventure in the Erg Chebbi–the vast expanse of sand dunes that line the nearby border with Algeria.

Like the rally drivers who used to charge close by here as they made their way between Paris and Dakar, most of the back-packers and affluent retirees race pass the village in their 4x4's and rented trucks. To-day, their destinations are the comfortable auberges and palatial hotels of Merzouga–from where they can be taken by camel or Land Rover into the dunes.

I came here in search of the raw desert, but being something of a hermit by nature and wanting to deepen my bond with Mother Gaia, I decided to stay here, setting about a project to renovate a ramshackle house.

After buying my property, I had little money to spend on refurbishment. But I've gradually taught myself how to turn a dilapidated skeleton of breezeblocks into something resembling a home.

The Berber people who've now settled in the village have accepted me like a member of their own family. Since the borders with our neighbours were closed, their days of roaming across the desert in search of food have ended.

Several of the young have helped me fit a roof to this place, as well as showing their talents at carpentry. Several of the women folk have introduced me to the art of camel hair weaving. As a result, I've been able to make a rug for myself, as well as a kaftan to provide protection against the cold winter nights.

In return for the villagers' kindness, I've set up a small school for the younger children, and also help the older folks learn a little French. Since I was born in Corsica, this is a happy way for me to share something of my native culture that helps my new neighbours sharpen their language skills.

Before I came to Morocco, I spent almost two years crossing central Asia, and then ventured into India. My yearning was always for places that allowed me to feel embraced by our mother, Gaia. I have sailed down the formidable sweep of the Volga, hitch-hiked my way across the Great Steppe, trekked high into the majestic Altai Mountains, and lost myself in the magnificent pine forests of Jammu. Along the way, I've met many people–and learned more than a few tricks in the art of survival.

When I came to Morocco, I was keen to put some of what I'd learned to good use, but I quickly discovered that the desert calls all who choose to converse with her to commit to her own multifarious methods for giving and taking life. I want to follow her rules as much as possible, but haven't yet completely managed to loosen all of my ties with the convenient habits of my youth.

Each month, I take my ageing Land Rover for a twenty mile run to Erfoud–the nearest town–where I stock up on vegetables, couscous, and other essentials.

When I arrived here, my house lacked electricity, and so I had no means for refrigerating food. But a well-shaded pit that I've hollowed out in a corner of my house provides cool storage for a time. My hope is to eventually cultivate a small vegetable plot, but my experiments with different crops have so far failed to yield little more than a few scrawny shoots of okra and a handful of feeble looking carrots. However, I'm sure that I'm making progress with what my imported soil, protective polytunnel and rudimentary irrigation system is able to produce.

Our water is drawn from the village well, which I reuse as much as I can. I ration my hair wash to one day in three, and always cook with water that I've used for cleaning.

I've also purchased a number of sheep, which I keep in a small enclosure that I've fenced off at the back of my house. My modest flock has started to produce young, and so I'm hopeful that I will soon be able to rely on a steady source of meat, as well as a supply of wool that I can sell in the town for a small profit.

While some might think my diet is meagre when compared with the three hearty meals that I used to enjoy when I lived in Europe, it's sufficient for my needs. I've fine-tuned my culinary skills since arriving in the village—creating what I like to think are tasty soups and tagines, concocted from whatever scraps and spices I might have in store. Perhaps I fool myself, but somehow everything always seems to taste better when it's cooked over an open fire—or, as I prefer to call it, my "outdoor oven".

I'm still learning how to make my way in this remote place, but I feel that I've come far since giving up my comfortable flat in Marseilles. I worked in that great metropolis for two years after leaving Ajaccio. Now, few things disturb the gentle rhythm of life that beats in the village.

The seasons come and go, of course, bringing their own share of gifts and adversity. At times, the valley on whose gentle slopes our homes are built has suddenly flooded with water, reminding us that nothing ever stays still for long in what visitors to our parts often believe is a dead landscape.

There are sufficient scrubs and even a few trees that survive the changing conditions, drawing moisture from the water that flows underground. This subterranean lifeline also supplies the village well.

I've never regretted choosing my current way of life–feeling at peace and more in touch with the Great Mother than I've ever done before. The pace of life here suits me, and I've no plans to return to the busyness of the city.

However, my gentle routine was recently interrupted by the appearance a couple of unexpected visitors. Tore and Monika–a couple of thirty-something travellers–had taken up temporary residence in my home.

Tore and Monika had arrived from Malmö, having completed a 3,000 kilometre road trip across Western Europe. Of course, they didn't set off with the intention of ending their journey in Tissardmine. Neither had their crossing of a continent been carried out in a matter of a few days.

෧෧

The pair had hoped that their trusty but unsuitable city-car would have taken them further along the dusty track to Merzouga, from where they intended to take a camel trip into the dunes. Unfortunately, their two-door hatchback wasn't up to the job of negotiating the bumps, stones and potholes of the unmade road from Erfoud, and it had come to an undignified stop just outside the village, when it had attempted to ride the contours of an unseen ditch.

Since my house lies on the edge of the village, Tore and Monika came to me before knocking on other doors, and were pleased to discover that I was a native of Corsica. Both had spent time in France when they were students, and so we could converse without difficulty.

"We wonder if you can help us?" Monika began. "Our car is stuck in a ditch, and we wondered if you know anyone who might be able to tow us out?"

I had a tow rope that I kept in my Land Rover and–with the help of a few willing volunteers from the village–took very little time to pull the Volvo free from its predicament.

The pair offered wide smiles and repeated wishes of thanks. But when Monika turned the key to start the ignition to set their trusted friend on its way again, rather than persuading the engine to settle into a reassuring purr, the starter motor let out an agonizing screech. The piercing cries continued in short bursts as Monika repeatedly tried to urge the troubled motor into action. After several failed attempts, the pair concluded that they had a problem.

I offered to take the couple to Merzouga, and to collect them from there several days later, by when they might have had a chance to arrange for a mechanic to take care of their vehicle. However, it was clear that they were at a loss to know what to do, and so I invited them to spend the night with me in Tissardmine.

"You're very welcome to spend a night or two here," I offered. "You'd need to sleep on the floor, but you'll be safe here. I can soon fix you something warm to eat."

Grateful for my suggestion, Tore and Monika proceeded to unpack the Volvo. I was staggered to see how much luggage they had brought with them—two fully packed rucksacks, a large four-wheeled trolley case, assorted walking shoes, an impressively equipped camera (complete with a tripod and a set of lenses of different kinds), matching *The North Face* branded hoodies, and of course—a pair of sleeping bags.

The couple seemed surprised at the small size and spartan furnishings of my abode, but attempted to hide their horror at the prospect of spending a night in such a place. They were less restrained in expressing their feelings when I proposed the menu for our meal.

Lamb was clearly off limits for these self-respecting vegetarians.

"We do not approve of killing animals," Monika announced firmly. "Being cruel to animals is not necessary for us to eat well."

I took the meat from their bowls, leaving them with a weak soup of sandy water and a scattering of locally gathered shrubs and herbs.

"It's difficult out here to get many vegetables," I attempted to explain. "Keeping animals is the only way the nomadic people manage to survive. Now people are less on the move, some are trying to discover what they might be able to grow in these unfriendly sands. But no one yet has been able to produce enough to feed their families."

I appreciated Tore and Monika's conviction, but I felt that I wanted to open their eyes a little to the hard reality of desert living. I explained that I and other villages did shop in the town, but with our meagre incomes, we had to complement the food we could afford with whatever we could produce ourselves.

"I tried being a vegetarian when I first arrived here," I went on. "But without spending all my money on food from the supermarket, I soon realised that I would have to make do with what Mother Nature provides. We look after our animals well, feeding them as best we can and giving them space to roam, but we have to survive."

My guests didn't appear to be persuaded by my argument, continuing their protests about the horror of slaughtering living creatures, and seeming to take pride in the stand that they'd adopted.

We finished our meal, and I then showed Monika and Tore the method that I used for washing, before pointing out areas outside the house where they could make their toilet. The pair seemed horrified at the conditions that they'd walked into, but feigning gratitude, they resolved to try to make the best of the situation.

The following morning, I rose many hours before the travellers, who had been exhausted by their previous day's adventure. When they awoke, I offered them some fruit for breakfast, and then proposed driving them to Merzouga. However, both felt they would like to spend another day in Tissardmine, if I would be happy to accommodate them or could suggest where else they might stay. I felt content to entertain them for a short while longer, and suggested that they might like me to show them the area.

I liked to spend time meditating on a fossil reef that had been exposed on one side of the village. Here, it was possible to see the imprints of sea creatures from different ages, whose histories were separated by millions of years. The sharp outcrop of the reef contrasted with the rocky slopes that fell away on one of its sides, and the pure sands that had been weathered by many millennia on the other.

I brought Monika and Tore to the reef, where I invited them to share my wonder at the unimaginable expanse of time over which this place had been created.

"Our lifespans are but a hair's breadth when compared with the life of this rock," I observed. "Yet Mother Gaia provides for each one of us, knowing that we have a vital role to play in her great design."

Monika and Tore stared at me as though I were deranged, but held their silence while I took my moment to meditate.

I then took them to an island of trees and bushes that marked the edge of the oasis. When the floodwaters came, this was the area that was inundated the most—being a natural basin that had been deepened by the repeated beating of water.

My visitors seemed surprised to see fig trees and acacias growing next to each other, in what was otherwise a barren landscape. I invited them to join me in sitting beside one of the many bushes that grew there, suggesting that we rest awhile and try to attune our hearts to whatever the plant wanted us to hear.

Monika and Tore must have thought that I had given leave to my senses, but they could see that I was sincere in my suggestion.

I had a strong feeling that the plant wanted to be left alone. It seemed to be saying that it felt crowded by the frenetic energy that our presence brought, and that it had suffered greatly at the hands of humans, since some of its branches had been torn from the ground to provide fodder for our animals.

I shared what I sensed the plant was saying with Tore and Monika. To my surprise, Monika said that she had attempted to follow my suggestion, though she did not know what to do. "I had a very vague feeling that we should go away," she remarked, "Almost as though the bush didn't have a good feeling toward people."

We moved on from the oasis, climbing a ridge that overlooked the village. There, we made for a place where we could survey the surrounds. As we walked, we reflected on our encounter with the bush.

"This sort of thing happens for me more and more," I offered. "As I spend more time sitting with nature and doing my best to connect with my heart, I'm sensing things that I wouldn't have imagined before."

My guests seemed curious to hear more about my experiences, and particularly what I believe plants want to say to us.

"I'm still discovering that," I admitted, "But for the most part, I think they just want to be heard and recognised as being alive. They may not have consciousness quite as we might experience it, but they seem to be aware and in tune with their environment."

"Are you suggesting that plants are conscious when we eat them?" asked Tore.

"Yes, I think they probably are," I replied, "And almost certainly when we uproot them from the ground–their source of nourishment."

Monika and Tore pondered this possibility as we walked, perhaps considering that eating vegetables might involve its own measure of cruelty–different from what animals might suffer maybe–but involving pain nonetheless.

When we arrived at the top of the ridge, we were able to observe the course of the river that fed the oasis, dry as it now was. The sheltered setting of the island of greenery was more obvious from here, and we could see twisted etchings in the desert, indicating the direction that the wind was carrying the sand.

We returned to my house and, following lunch, made time for a siesta. When they awoke, Monika and Tore seemed much more reflective than when they'd arrived.

"How do you manage to live in a place like this?" questioned Tore. "In our country, we have everything we need–refrigerators, power showers, patio heaters. We can entertain ourselves at the theatre one night, then take in a jazz gig the next. When our car breaks down, we know that it can be attended to within a matter of hours. When we don't want to drive, comfortable trams and fast buses allow us to get almost anywhere.

"Here, you have nothing—no supermarket, no electricity, no running water. What you eat is not enough to feed a child, and a cold floor serves as your bed."

I left Tore's question unanswered for a moment, though I never doubted how I would respond.

"What you say is true, as I know from the time when I lived in Marseille," I began. "There are times when I would like to chill out with a bottle of wine and a movie, or be able to while away a few hours in the city library. But I feel very drawn to where I am now. This is the best university that I could wish for to learn about the wonder of being alive and being part of an incredible universe.

"Gradually, I'm coming home to playing the part that Mother Gaia has ordained for me in the impossibly complex web that creates, sustains, and ultimately ends all life. I'm learning to trust her for her bountiful provision, and every day am captivated by new wonders.

"When I lived in the city, I had money and a smart apartment. There, I made provision for my future, building up a small pension and making plans for the journeys I would take when I had free time. Now I have all the time that I need, and every day is a wonderful adventure."

Tore and Monika listened carefully. "We are on an adventure too," Monika ventured. "We made plans about where we would go, but now find ourselves in a place that we hadn't expected to visit."

Monika went on to explain that they intended to return to Sweden soon, where they would pick up their careers, and perhaps start a family. Through their trip—by meeting people from different cultures and from the experiences that came their way—they hoped that they would become more rounded people. They had no concept of contemplating a future that was anything other than "normal".

We enjoyed sharing conversation for the remainder of the day, exchanging anecdotes about our travel experiences and finding common ground in some of the issues that we were passionate about. We'd all been members of EYFA—a network of environmentalists—and each professed our love of the Earth and deep wish for people to stop abusing her.

The following morning, I drove my visitors to Merzouga, agreeing to return there to collect them several days later.

They took a camel trip, as they'd planned, staying overnight in a Berber camp amid the dunes. There, they saw spectacular sunsets and marvelled at brilliant night skies. They took long walks across the dunes, and reflected on what we'd discussed at Tissardmine. They'd even fasted from eating for a whole day, and apparently spent many hours talking about their future.

The two were still very contemplative when I collected them, saying very little during our forty-minute drive back to Tissardmine. Their car had been repaired during their stay in the dunes, and it took them little time to fill it with their miscellaneous kit, ready to continue on their journey.

Before we said our goodbyes, Monika took out a small parcel from her rucksack, which I later discovered contained a beautifully polished fossil. Handing the package to me, she held my arms, and said with what I could see was sincere intent, "We would like you to have this small gift as a mark of our gratitude. Not only for your generosity in providing us with food and shelter when we needed help, but for all that you have taught us.

"We thought carefully about what you told us while we were at the dunes. We are going back to Sweden, but not to our jobs in Malmö. We plan to set up a retreat centre in the north, where the forest will provide our wood for fuel, and we'll cultivate our own vegetables. We will never forget our time in Morocco. You have changed our lives."

We embraced, promising to keep contact. Then I watched the couple depart for Erfoud, leaving a stream of dust in their wake.

Afterword

The story of the *Old woman and the pilgrim* beautifully conveys its message, contrasting the simple but peaceable existence of the woman with the ostensibly comfortable but enslaved life of the pilgrim.

The vignette of the pilgrim's encounter with the woman is set within a frame story that warns that people get the type of leader they deserve–those who squabble and seek material and selfish gain would do well to remember that they are bound to a continuous cycle of oppression. There is no escape from the clutches of the world for those that choose this path– no salvation or spiritual riches to be found.

The old woman sees through the supposed attractions of the material world, knowing that what she holds in her heart is far more precious than to live in a city that claims to offer everything.

The pilgrim presumably embarked on his journey expecting to receive enrichment for his soul. He may have expected to find enlightenment at the sacred place that was his original destination. Instead, it is after becoming lost that he unexpectedly stumbles upon what he might consider to be an unpromising place–and it's here that he's taught an important truth.

The old woman shows hospitality, also willingly taking on a parental role to capture some serpents when the pilgrim admits his fear about hunting them. She is sustained by what Nature provides, and doesn't complain about this. Her lifestyle and wisdom hint at the authentic life of an ascetic, contrasting with the pretend asceticism of the city-dwelling traveller.

In this story, we are not told whether the pilgrim ultimately takes on board what the old woman has shown him, or whether he chooses to go back to the life that he once knew. What we can be certain of is that the woman will not trade the life that she knows is best.

The history of Abou Neeut and Abou Neeuten

A poor but holy man named Abou Neeut–which means "of a single purpose"–was once contemplating his situation. Destitute and without hope of finding prosperity in his own country, he resolved to journey to a foreign place, where he might discover a better life. Duly, he gathered his only possession–a single shekel– and set out on his journey.

After a short while, Abou Neeut came upon another traveller, who was set upon the same mission. They engaged in lively conversation for sometime, before resolving to become companions in their joint quest. Deciding to pool their resources, for which they would have equal share, Abou Neeut agreed to become the common purse holder, which now included nine shekels that had been contributed by his fellow adventurer.

Strange to behold, this newfound friend went by a similar name to Abou Neeut, Abou Neeuten—which means "one who has double intentions".

The two journeyed together for some days, battling against exhaustion and great hardships. After ten days, they came upon a bustling city. Passing through one of the great gates that gave entry to the city, the companions were soon accosted by a beggar, pleading that they might show him some generosity.

"Give alms to the poor, and you shall be rewarded tenfold," uttered the beggar, recalling the promise of Scripture. Affected by the poor man's distress, Abou Neeut took one shekel from the shared purse, which he joyfully handed to the beggar.

"Allah be praised!" cried the beggar, "Blessings be upon you, my good friend!"

Despite Abou Neeut's assurance that this gift was rightfully offered, his companion accused him of being reckless, angrily decrying his extravagance.

Abou Neeuten now determined that Abou Neeut was unfit to accompany him, and so demanded back his contribution to the purse, such that he might continue his journey alone. Abou Neeut consented to his request, whereupon the two men set off on their separate ways.

Now without a shekel, Abou Neeut retreated to the city's main mosque, where he hoped that he might receive charity from a passing believer. He entrusted his fate to Allah, confident that he had been brought to his current situation because of divine will.

One night and one day passed by, but not a single stranger offered charity to Abou Neeut. As another evening approached and being overcome with hunger, Abou Neeut proceeded to leave the grounds of the mosque, hopeful that he might find another place where he might be blessed by an act of kindness.

Proceeding slowly through the city's narrow passageways, Abou Neeut eventually sighted the walls of a great house, from which a servant was throwing out the bones and crumbs that had been left over from his master's meal. Filled with gratitude, Abou Neeut quickly gathered the sparse leftovers, eagerly taking nourishment from them. Raising his arms in praise to the Almighty, he shouted aloud his gratitude for this precious gift.

The servant who observed this was astonished, and proceeded to tell his master what he had seen. Now the owner of this house, a wealthy merchant, was a pious man, who took compassion when he heard about Abou Neeut's display of gratitude. He resolved to reward this simple example of faith, commanding that his servant take a purse of ten shekels to him, that these might help Abou Neeut along his way.

Filled with greed, the servant held back one shekel for himself, giving the other nine to Abou Neeut. Abou Neeut then prostrated himself before the walls of the house, calling praises to Allah, and wishing good tidings to his most generous benefactor.

However, when Abou Neeut counted the contents of the purse, he wondered why only nine coins were contained therein, remembering that the Lord repays those who show charity to others by tenfold.

The master of the house, a wealthy merchant, had observed the scene from his garden. Being deeply affected by Abou Neeut's deep faith, he gave instruction to his servant to bring him into the house, such that he might afford him hospitality.

Abou Neeut was warmly welcomed, offered a bath, clean clothes, and refreshment. The merchant asked Abou Neeut about his history, curious to know the circumstance in which he had come to give up his last shekel. Abou Neeut related the full details of what had befallen him.

Taking pity, his host welcomed Abou Neeut to stay in his house for some time, that he might fully restore his strength, and then be ready to continue his journey.

It happened that it was the season for believers to make accounts of what they owned, from which amount they should give up one tenth for the glory of Allah. Duly, the merchant computed the value of his estate, then chose to award one tenth of his entire wealth to Abou Neeut, recommending that he set up a store, such that he might try his hand as a merchant.

Filled with gratitude, Abou Neeut acted faithfully on his generous host's advice. Within a short time, he had achieved considerable success with his new business adventure. Following several years, Abou Neeut earned a considerable reputation amongst his peers, and had built up an appreciable stock of goods.

One day, Abou Neeut noticed a wretched man who was appealing for alms outside of his warehouse. True to his nature, Abou Neeut immediately instructed his servant to invite the man into his house, such that he might offer him hospitality.

When the man was brought in, Abou Neeut immediately recognised him as Abou Neeuten, his one time companion who had been quick to abandon him.

But rather than berate his brother for his past deed, Abou Neeut took great pity on his current situation. The kindly host willed that his servants bring Abou Neeuten fine clothes, prepare a warm bath for him, and ready a comfortable room for his stay.

Over supper, Abou Neeut enquired of his guest, "My brother, do you not recognise who I am?" Abou Neeuten could not see that the very man that he had left penniless was now sitting before him. "No, my generous host," he replied, "I do not believe that we have met before."

Upon this admission Abou Neeut revealed his true identity, and proceeded to relate the course of events that had led him to his current good fortune.

"I remain your brother," Abou Neeut asserted. "I haven't forgotten our agreement, and remain faithful to honouring my commitment to you. A half of everything that I own is yours."

Abou Neeut was quick to compute the value of his possessions, and wasted no time in sharing his worth with Abou Neeuten.

As Abou Neeut had done before him, Abou Neeuten began a small enterprise, which after sometime, achieved some success and reputation. The two men dwelt close by each other for several years, trading well and enjoying comfortable lives.

However, Abou Neeuten eventually grew restless with his routine, and appealed to Abou Neeut that they might set off on a new adventure together. Abou Neeut was reluctant to leave behind the satisfied life that he enjoyed. "Why should we leave behind our comfortable homes, where we have many friends and make a good profit?" he enquired. "We have everything that we need, and will surely not want for anything if we stay where we are."

But Abou Neeuten could not be persuaded to depart from his plan, and continued his appeals to Abou Neeut. Eventually, Abou Neeut relented, agreeing to join his impatient brother on a new journey. The pair gathered provisions for their expedition, loaded their camels, and left behind their businesses. They then set out on a path for the great city of Mosul.

The companions' journey took them along the same desert road that they had started upon before. Abou Neeuten assured his near-namesake that, before long, they would encounter many wonderful adventures together, and need have no cause for anxiety about where they might seek enjoyment.

Ten days following their departure, the pair came upon a deep well, close to which they saw fit to set up their camp for the night.

When morning arrived, Abou Neeut offered to be let down into the well, such that he might fetch water more easily than by drawing it from the top. Abou Neeuten received the water that was brought up to the ground, and readied the camels for departure. However, rather than assisting his companion to climb out from the well, Abou Neeuten took out his knife and cut through the rope, leaving Abou Neeut to an uncertain fate. Abou Neeuten now counted his former companion's possessions as his own.

With the caravan gone, Abou Neeut reflected upon his old friend's act of treachery. Remembering his faith, he determined that it must be Allah's Will that he again found himself in such a perilous predicament. "Mighty Allah, I do not know why You have brought me here, but may I always be faithful to Your Will!" he cried.

For one night and one day, Abou Neeut rested at the foot of the dark hole, unable to discern a way of freeing himself from that foreboding place. During the course of the following night, perhaps around midnight, two afreets came to convene by the well.

Well enough for Abou Neeut to hear, one afreet turned excitedly to the other, and exclaimed, "I am filled with perfect joy. For now I have succeeded in possessing the princess of Mosul. No one can drive me away, but for knowledge of a secret that none can surely learn! My hold can only be broken by one who sprinkles an infusion of wormwood over the feet of the princess during the reciting of prayers at the Great Mosque of Mosul!"

"I too have come upon great fortune," cried the second afreet. "I have come into the possession of a vast hoard of treasure, the like of which has never been known in any kingdom. This is buried under a blue-earth mound near Mosul, and cannot be found unless the talisman that guards it is discovered. This requires that a cock of pure white be sacrificed over the top of the mound, whereupon the dripping of its blood will cause the earth to open. I wager that no one will ever discover such a secret!"

Following their discourse, the two afreet took flight, leaving Abou Neeut to contemplate what he had heard.

Abou Neeut awoke early the next morning, disturbed by the sound of men, whose caravan was passing. One of their number was let down into the well to gather water, where he was surprised to encounter Abou Neeut. Not wishing to reveal the true reason for his situation, Abou Neeut explained that he had accidentally fallen into the well at night.

After being taken back into the safety of the camp, Abou Neeut begged that he might be allowed to join the caravan on their continued journey to Mosul, as his own companions had departed without noticing that he was missing.

The hospitable travellers agreed to Abou Neeut's request, and ensured that he was given adequate refreshment before they set off on the next stage of their journey.

When the party reached Mosul, Abou Neeut was surprised to see many people rushing about, making haste for what he assumed was a great event. Asking a passerby what was the cause of this commotion, he was told that the people were rushing to witness the execution of a physician in the great square beside the palace. Like many who had tried before him, the physician had failed to relieve the sultan's daughter of an evil spirit that had possessed her.

Upon hearing this, Abou Neeut bade farewell to the travellers who had so generously conveyed him, and made quickly to the palace, seeking an urgent audience with the sultan. After making the customary acts of servility, the newcomer was received by the sultan to explain his case.

Like the many who had preceded him, Abou Neeut pleaded with the sultan that he be allowed an attempt to heal his daughter. The sultan consented to the request, and also to his plea that the condemned physician be spared his life should Abou Neeut succeed in relieving the princess of her torment. However, this request was granted only on condition that should he fail, Abou Neeut would be beheaded alongside the physician, for both would have been shown to be pretenders in their art.

Abou Neeut made a further request, that he be allowed access to the princess during prayer time the following Friday, reasoning that the prayers of many would assist him in his task. Duly, the sultan gave orders that all citizens should observe their duties at the mosque on that holy day. The physician was escorted from the square to a cell in the palace, where Abou Neeut was also afforded temporary accommodation.

When the holy day arrived, Abou Neeut was granted access to the princess's quarters. Entering her room, he saw her slumped on a couch, shivering and

seemingly overcome with something like a night terror.

Abou Neeut proceeded to sprinkle an infusion of
wormwood that he had obtained the day before, covering the princess's feet with the powerful concoction.

No sooner had he completed this task, than the
princess began to cry out loudly, calling for her attendants to help her dress and make her toilet. As
though awakening fully from a dream, her shivering
stopped and she regained a luminous complexion.

Overjoyed, her attendants rushed quickly to the
sultan, beseeching him to come to his daughter's
apartment. The sultan was astonished to see that his
daughter had fully recovered, and promised Abou
Neeut whatever reward he desired. He freed the imprisoned physician, ordered a great celebration, and
offered gifts to the poor.

For his reward, Abou Neeut asked that he might
have the hand of the princess in marriage, for he had
become besotted with her.

The sultan retreated to consult with his viziers regarding Abou Neeut's request. They advised that
Abou Neeut should return the following morning,
when the sultan would give his decision.

Following further deliberation, the viziers proposed
that no suitor could be worthy to wed the princess,
unless he had sufficient means to support her in a way
that was worthy of her rank. They counselled that

Abou Neeut should be presented with a display of treasures whose value his wealth must at least equal. Should he fail to prove his worth, he could not be considered a suitable husband for the sultan's daughter.

When the decision was put to Abou Neeut the following morning, and he was shown the treasures whose value his wealth was expected to rival, Abou Neeut did not hesitate to promise that he would offer a dowry worth ten times as much as that he had seen.

The court was astonished, since it was known that no prince's wealth could rival that of the sultan's.

Abou Neeut showed no concern for their doubting, but rather went from the palace, making quickly to the poultry market, where he purchased the finest white cock that he could find.

After dark, Abou Neeut set off alone with the cock, coming to the blue-earth mound that he had heard the afreet speak about. As the sun started to rise the following morning, Abou Neeut cut the throat of the cock, allowing its blood to drip on top of the mound.

No sooner had he done this, than the ground around him shook more violently than the wildest earthquake, opening a large chasm where the mound had once stood. As the afreet had described, untold of treasures were brought to light in the gathering rays of the rising sun.

Abou Neeut returned quickly to the city, where he procured ten camels, each laden with two large panniers. Returning to the site of the mound, he gathered the hoard, filling every pannier with the brightest of jewels and purest gold. He then led the train carrying his remarkable cargo back to the grand courtyard at the heart of the palace.

When he arrived, Abou Neeut unloaded the treasures, which he formed into a most elaborate display, then begged that the sultan should come to meet him. When the sultan saw the treasures, he was amazed. Consulting his viziers once more, he enquired what he should now do. Without hesitating, his advisers unanimously recommended that Abou Neeut should be offered the hand of the sultan's daughter in marriage. A fine wedding was soon arranged, and Abou Neeut became a well-loved member of the royal household.

Abou Neeut equipped himself so well in his new role, that he quickly earned the highest respect from his noble father-in-law. Abou Neeut's great protestation of faith and wise counsel soon convinced the sultan that, for some three days per week, he should permit his son-in-law to give audience and make judgements in his place.

After several years, there came a wretched man to the palace, begging for alms. Abou Neeut instructed his macebearers to lead the man to him. Looking kindly upon the man, Abou Neeut saw at once that it was his former companion, Abou Neeuten.

Unaffected by anger for the treachery that Abou Neeuten had shown to him, and not drawn to take revenge, Abou Neeut was moved only with compassion on seeing the sorry state that his former friend had come to.

As he had done before, Abou Neeut offered a steaming bath, fine clothes, and a place of rest for the weary figure. Over dinner, Abou Neeut enquired whether Abou Neeuten knew who he was. "No, Your Excellency, I cannot say that I know anything of your past," Abou Neeuten replied.

Abou Neeut then revealed his true identity, relating the story that had brought him to his current position. "Your leaving me in the well was decreed by fate," Abou Neeut explained, "For without the intelligence that I overheard from the afreets, I would not have come to my current situation."

Abou Neeut repeated his pledge to share what he had with Abou Neeuten, but his jealous guest rejoined, "Since the well offered such good fortune for you, then surely it will do likewise for me!" Abou Neeuten then made haste for the well, into which he lowered himself, waiting for the afreets' return.

At night, the afreets again convened beside the well, within clear earshot of Abou Neeuten.

"Woe to this wretched well!" exclaimed one of the pair. "For it was here that knowledge of the spell that broke my possession of the princess was discovered. O wretched well!"

With similar dismay, the second afreet cried, "And it was at this well too that the secret for acquiring my treasure was discovered! O wretched well, how you have ruined us!"

At this, the afreet resolved to fill-in the well, such that it might not bring further misfortune to them. Quickly, the hole was filled with stones, and Abou Neeuten was crushed beneath them.

When Abou Neeuten failed to return to the palace after some days, Abou Neeut realised that misfortune might have befallen him. He therefore commanded that the well be dug up. In due course, Abou Neeuten's bones were discovered.

Abou Neeut concluded that it was Abou Neeuten's malicious spirit that caused his own destruction. He lamented that all should be protected from envy, because the envious are led to their own destruction.

Now in old age, the ailing sultan expressed his wish that Abou Neeut should be his heir, even though his daughter had two older sisters whose husbands might lay claim to the throne.

The sultan's wishes were honoured following his death.

Down by the Yarra

It's fair to say that Debs' and my relationship has at times been painfully strained. As my elder sister, she hasn't always been able to easily accept the fortunes that have come my way, although most of what I've achieved has involved anything but luck.

We often argued when we were growing up. But our famous tiffs always ended with hugs and tears, and promises that we would always support each other. While at times Debs nearly drove me to despair, I was sure that I'd always stand by her, and do my best to help her make a success of her life.

Unfortunately, my sister has never been able to deal with her problem of jealousy. Perhaps it's an insecurity thing; perhaps it's just pride. Whatever the reason, she's never been able to accept that her little sister

Anna has occasionally fared better than her. Inevitably, this has often led to her bemoaning what she believes are her inadequacies and unlucky lot.

Her jealousy toward me became especially obvious as we went through our teenage years. I earned better grades in my exams, and even on one occasion was honoured with a school prize. I became leader of my patrol in Girl Guides Australia, where she never progressed through the rank-and-file, and later I became a school prefect–a role that Debs felt she was destined for, but was cheated from having the chance to add to her resume.

Then there was the matter of the North Melbourne Community Prize. This was the first time when I realised that Debs wasn't satisfied to simply complain when she saw me being lauded and moving on with my activities, bewailing why it wasn't her who received all the accolades and opportunities. This particular incident introduced me to another side of my sister, one in which she displayed far greater skill and intelligence than me–her ability to manipulate and denigrate.

The Community Prize was awarded each year to a small group or an individual who, in the view of the neighbourhood council's judges, had made the greatest contribution to the life and wellbeing of the community. I had involved myself with several projects since I joined the Guides, and a few of these had involved Debs. Her contribution was always minimal, but my friends and I let her believe that her efforts were appreciated.

For our summer project, I proposed to the six chums in my patrol that we set ourselves up as a litter collecting crew, making a weekly effort to clear garbage from the park beside our clubhouse. We sported high-viz tabards, and weren't shy about publicising what we were doing. Our invitation was for folks to add a few cents to the collection box that we'd organised, to show their support for our activities. We'd then use the money that we'd collected to treat some of the old folks in the neighbourhood to a Sunday lunch at the clubhouse. For this part of our plan, we also took on the roles of cooks and waitresses.

Debs was keen to be included in our team, although she wasn't a member of my patrol. Not wanting to hurt her feelings, I agreed that she could join us, although her involvement proved to be more in name rather than being distinguished by much physical action.

When the prize committee met to consider the various projects that were vying for the coveted award, Debs suddenly became more enthusiastic about the venture, volunteering to be our spokesman at the presentation that the committee would see before making their decision. The group and I were astounded by her insistence to be our representative, but knowing that she would retreat into a sulk if we didn't let her have her way, we reluctantly agreed.

Debs spoke well on our behalf, but I couldn't believe how devious she was in portraying the project as being largely her own idea.

The committee seemed very impressed with what we had achieved, and decided that we deserved to receive the prize. I imagine that someone on the committee had been impressed by Debs' performance, because she was invited to collect the prize, and was individually mentioned in the committee's citation for its decision to choose our project for the award.

Looking back now, the whole episode seems farcical. But at the time, I was outraged that my own sister had claimed credit for the work that had been largely left to my pals and me. Still, this was Debs–and I resolved at the time to not get into a fight with her over who should have collected the prize.

There were other initiatives that Debs took the glory for, which I won't elaborate on now. In truth, I don't think that anyone who knew her really believed that she was quite the supergirl that she made out to be.

When it came to sitting exams, this was one activity in which we are each judged according to our own merits. Debs took her VCE exams two years before me, but she failed to impress anyone with her grades.

She had hoped to be offered a place to study pharmacology at the University of Melbourne, but had to settle for a diploma course at the Flinders College when she didn't obtain what we call an ATAR rating–a grade that's needed to qualify for a degree placement. I'm sure that she had the ability to make it to uni if she'd wanted, but her final year at high school involved more time eyeing up the guys at nightclubs than getting familiar with her textbooks.

I fared much better with my final grades–managing to be offered a place at the Melbourne Medical School, where I studied for a degree in medicine. It had always been my dream to become a nurse, but I hadn't closed my eyes to the possibility of taking the long road to becoming a doctor.

Debs was furious with envy at my acceptance by such an esteemed school, offering her words of congratulation through gritted teeth.

"I've heard that it was a particularly easy year," she sneered. "And of course, there are far more places available for people who want to study medicine than there are for pharmacologists."

Such comments were typical of my sister, and I was usually able to let them pass. It did annoy me that she was so ungracious about my success, when I'd always tried to support her and celebrate the good things that came to her. When we were younger, we made a pledge to look after each other whatever paths our lives took. I hadn't forgotten my promise, being willing to share what I could with her if ever the need arose.

I worked hard at my degree, and perhaps Debs started to make more of an effort with her diploma too, because she was awarded with a merit grade when she graduated from her course. She took up a post as an assistant to a pharmacist soon after. This gave her a steady income, which I was still many years away from achieving.

While I was living on campus, I saw my sister far less frequently than before. She was busying herself in her bachelorette life–sleeping around with guys, and making a nuisance of herself in the cocktail bars and tap bars of St. Kilda.

For a time, she dated a player with the North Melbourne Football Club, the Aussie rules team that we'd both been mad about since our early teens. She was keen to let everyone know that she was shacked up with a member of the Kangas, but didn't approve of his reluctance to join her on her nightly excursions downtown. He became suspicious that she was two-timing him, and following a blistering row, the pair parted company.

This was one of several occasions when she came running to my door. I always did my best to console her, and would offer her a bed for as long as she needed it. These were times when Debs temporally remembered our promise to stand by each other, offering assurances of the kind, "I'll be there for you one day, sweetheart, I swear that I will!"

Suddenly finding herself without a boyfriend, Debs soon started to complain about the unfairness of her life. As she was want to do, she denounced the good fortune that had befallen me—my steady progress through medical school, my lack of crises to deal with, and the fact that I had recently become smitten with a man whom she felt was far too good for me.

Life wasn't all plain sailing for me, of course. My studies involved long hours in the school, and now also required me undertaking practical exercises at the Royal Women's Hospital. I struggled to pay my bills, taking work at an all-night grocery store in order to top up my income. My relationship with Liam, my new man, was the first chance for romance that I'd had in several years, and we were still finding our way with each other.

Liam was older than me. He'd already set on a career, having landed a job downtown as a loans specialist at the ANZ bank. He had much more free time than I did, and had a disposable income that needed to be spent. When I was running late at the hospital, it would be Debs who greeted him when he drove to my place after finishing work.

It's obvious to me now that, sooner or later, my double-dealing sister would find a way to persuade Liam to enjoy some of the city's nightspots with her. Perhaps I had left him hanging around too much, or perhaps I had over-estimated how much our relationship meant to him. Whatever the truth, Debs took no more than three weeks after taking up residence in my apartment to begin dating Liam.

They carried on in clandestine fashion for several months, keeping their blossoming affair away from my attention. I believed that Liam's love for me was growing, and I felt certain that he was close to asking me to marry him. Instead, I woke up one morning to read a letter that he'd left by my bedside, quickly discovering that both he and Debs had fled the apartment.

Debs had left a letter too, informing me that she'd been sleeping with my boyfriend for the past six months, and had grown to hate my pretentious way of life. She said that she thought we'd moved far apart, and that she didn't expect to spend more time with me any time soon.

Naturally, I was devastated by Liam and Debs' deceit. I couldn't understand how I might have offended either of them, nor why Debs had built up a perception of me as a gloating braggart. I'd never wanted to do any more than to be a good sister to her, and to be faithful in my love for Liam.

With my exams approaching, I had to keep going with my work as best I could, though my only free time at home was spent cowering on my bed in a pool of tears.

Some of my friends on campus helped me come through that terrible time. I had sunk to such a low point that I even considered giving up my studies. By some miracle, I scraped through my exams, and then was able to regain my self-esteem in stages.

I didn't hear from Debs, as she'd promised. Liam also made himself unavailable to speak to me when I tried reaching him at the bank, and so I had to come to terms with the fact that our relationship really was over.

Despite how she'd treated me, I continued to worry about my sister. I wanted her to know that I wished her no harm, and didn't see myself to be any better than her. I reasoned that her actions had been prompted by jealousy, and that perhaps behind her strong facade, she might really be as insecure as me.

Months went by without a word from Debs, and I dedicated myself to my studies. Having now completed my first degree, I had started my Doctor of Medicine training, still spending much of my time in the hospital. I continued working under the supervision of experienced consultants at the hospital. After a time, under their close observation, I was given opportunities to treat real patients.

On one particularly busy night, I was surprised to see a patient being hurriedly wheeled into the emergency room where I was on duty. Having been involved in what I was told was a horrendous road accident, the young woman was unconscious, and her face was badly scarred and covered with blood. I realised straight away that my sister's life was in grave danger.

Almost disbelieving the situation that was unfolding in front of me, I robotically followed the instructions that were given to me by the supervising consultant. The Advanced Life Support team made several attempts to administer CPR to Debs, but the graph on the intensive care unit screen continued to register a steady line.

"I think we might have lost her," the consultant sighed, "But I'm not giving up just yet."

Hearing his words, I could no longer help myself from bursting into tears. One of my colleagues did her best to comfort me. When she learned that it was my own sister who was lying on the treatment table, the consultant asked if I wanted to be relieved.

I motioned that I wanted to continue, feeling that I had to play whatever part I could in our effort to save my sister.

"She's going to come through if I've got anything to do with it," the consultant tried to reassure me. But the heart trace line on the ICU monitor showed no sign of moving from its level trajectory. "Get ready for another go with the defibrillator," ordered the consultant.

The ALS team tried again to jolt Debs' heart back into life, but by now, I was certain that she was dead.

Instinctively, and against all normal conventions, I rushed to kiss my sister on the cheek. Crouching by her side and clutching her hand, I whispered through my tears, "I love you, Debs. I'm still with you, still by your side. Please don't die on me yet, old girl!"

What happened next amazed even the consultant. The ECG line jerked into a familiar zigzag, and Debs' heart began beating once more. She had two broken legs, and was still unconscious, but hope returned that she was going to be all right.

❧

It took Debs several weeks before she came out of her coma, and several months more before she was able to walk. When she was eventually discharged from The Royal Women's, I took it upon myself to nurse my sister at my apartment.

As she adjusted to her new surroundings and came to appreciate that I had been among those in the emergency room who had helped save her life, she sought to make amends for her long silence, tearfully apologising for the way that she had absconded with Liam.

It was not a time for being angry with my sister, and I repeated my promise to share what I had with her. It turned out that her relationship with Liam had lasted no more than a year. She'd had other boyfriends since then, though remained unhappy in her job.

Debs told me that she had had the most unusual experience while she'd been in the emergency room. "I felt as though I were fully conscious," she said, "But seemed to be floating, as it were, looking down on everything from someplace close to the ceiling.

"I could see you standing beside my body, heard the consultant promising you that I was going to come through, and saw you take my hands and gently kiss me.

"It was when you told me not to die that I found myself having to decide whether I was going to make another go of this life, or give up the ghost. In that moment, it wasn't clear to me why I should return. But I saw you crying and didn't want to leave you alone, and so I chose to come back to my body."

I'd read that most people who remember experiences like Debs' were often determined to make great changes to their lives when they came back to their normal senses. This wasn't the first time that an out of body experience had been reported by a patient saved in our emergency room, and I'm sure that it won't be the last.

Debs stayed with me for several months. As she regained her strength, she made herself useful around the home, keeping the place clean, and running errands for me when my duty roster absorbed me for virtually all of my waking hours.

I was sure that Debs had turned a corner since her ordeal, but it turned out that this particular cat had kept a few of her old spots.

Debs' jealousy toward me began to reveal itself once more, firstly through her grumbling at my supposed strength of character to withstand the various challenges that were put to me, and then declaring her envy for the good career in medicine that I seemed destined for.

I tried to encourage her to pick up with new studies–possibly to apply herself to a degree course, or to work at qualifying as a teacher, which was something that she'd spoken about in the past.

Debs made some efforts to explore options that might be open to her, and seemed to calm her aggression toward me when I offered to help fund any course that she committed herself to.

She did set about a degree, and later went on to train as a teacher. Finally, she achieved a professional status that she felt proud about. I naturally showered her with congratulations and praises–which were genuinely felt. I hoped that she would now see that I had always considered her to be my equal.

When my own training came to an end, I committed to working in the hospital for only five days each week. This gave me time to embark on another project that I was passionate about–offering palliative care to the elderly. I used to visit several old folks who had been diagnosed with terminal conditions, and who'd expressed a wish to be cared for in their homes, rather than spending their final days in a hospice or home for the sick.

This was difficult work, but I felt very drawn to offering my time to share company with people who rarely met others. I worked especially with those who lived alone—usually those who'd lost a partner or who didn't have a family to support them.

Debs had moved out from my apartment, although we met regularly for coffee in one of our favourite bistros near the Yarra River. We gossiped about people we knew—as sisters do—and often reminisced about experiences that we'd shared while we were growing up. I talked to Debs about virtually everything that occupied my time—which I confess included sharing the odd confidence about my appointments with my elderly friends.

One old man that I'd grown quite fond of had just passed away. When his will was revealed, it turned out that he wanted to leave a large part of his estate to me. I hadn't realised how much our conversations meant to him, but I felt very embarrassed to think about accepting his bequest.

Following discussion with his executor, my suggestion to allow a variation to his will was accepted his other beneficiaries. I proposed taking only a small token from the estate, leaving the remainder of the share that had been allotted to me to be divided among the other interested parties.

When I told Debs what had transpired, she was appalled by what she saw as my stupidity. "How can you be so foolish, giving up what for some of us is a small fortune?" she berated me. "The old guy clearly wanted you to have his lolly, and yet you've gone straight against his wishes!"

I tried to justify my position to Debs, explaining that I had offered to accept a token gift from the estate in honour of my friend's wishes. However, my sister clearly didn't share my point of view.

In disclosing the affairs about the will, I had inadvertently given Debs an idea. She seemed interested to learn how I'd come so close to making a tidy sum of dollars. She was convinced that she could achieve the same.

When we next met at our regular haunt by the Yarra, Debs revealed that she had started a weekend job–delivering pharmacy prescriptions for the housebound. Within a couple of months, she had begun offering companionship for some of her customers, being invited into their homes to share coffee. By this means, she was able to determine the marital and family status of the people whom she visited.

Debs claimed that she had become particularly friendly with an elderly gentleman, who had become paralysed after suffering a stroke. Debs told no one other than me about her visits, which I felt sure her bosses would not look favourably upon were they to get wind of her antics. When I attempted to question the morality of what she was doing, she simply replied that she was wasn't being negligent in her responsibility to deliver prescriptions, and was additionally giving her own time in the interests of enriching her customers' otherwise miserable lives.

Even with me, Debs was secretive about her meetings with her preferred client. She denied spending any more than an hour at a time with him, but I began to wonder whether she was being entirely truthful.

One night, I was awoken by a phone call from the Victoria Police. Debs had been arrested on suspicion of murder, and wanted my help to find a good lawyer to represent her.

I learned that she had called for an ambulance while visiting her client earlier in the day, claiming to have found that he had been asphyxiated after taking an overdose of warfarin. She claimed that she had found a spare key to the house, letting herself in when she received no reply as she'd tried to deliver the dead man's medicine. Finding the man lying lifeless, she'd called for an ambulance.

However, her story didn't fully add up–the police wanted to know how she knew where to find the spare key, and why she hadn't reported her inability to get a reply from the man to her manager. What's more, several neighbours had seen a woman that matched Debs' description running away from the house the previous night. It had also come to light that the deceased man had recently changed his will to name Debs as his sole beneficiary.

Given that she was considered a threat to vulnerable people, Debs was refused bail. Her lawyer is working with her to prepare her defence, but if she is found guilty of the crime for which she has been charged, I fear that my days of standing by her may soon be over.

Debs' trial begins next week, two days after the ceremony at which I'll be presented with my Doctor of Medicine degree.

Afterword

The story of *Abou Neeut and Abou Neeuten* seems to present an unambiguous conclusion–that piety and truth always ultimately triumph over evil intention. This is a theme that's picked up in many fairy stories and folklore–for example, in the Grimm brothers' tale of *The Two Travellers*. Abou Neeut remains faithful both to Allah and to his promise to his companion, even in the face of great adversity.

There are some beautiful vignettes in this story, such as Abou Neeut's gratitude for receiving the crumbs thrown out by the servant of the rich merchant. We are reminded that material wealth does not matter–only the attitude that a person demonstrates in the differing circumstances that they might find themselves in.

The contrast could not be starker between Abou Neeut's remaining grateful and trusting that Allah will look after his every need, and Abou Neeuten, who cannot be satisfied even when he is twice rescued from miserable situations and offered hospitality and riches that should comfortably satisfy his needs.

The test presented to Abou Neeut is one that's well-known in both Islamic and Christian Scripture– that one who gives freely to the poor will themselves enjoy riches tenfold, or *many times*, greater. This reward need not be one that's described in material terms, but by a nourishment of the soul and the bliss that follows from leading a godly life.

The similar names of Abou Neeut and Abou Neeuten suggest that they might represent two sides of the human character, or perhaps more probably, the choice that we have between following a righteous path or one driven by selfish motive. In the footnotes to his translation, Sir Richard Burton explains that the two names have often been mistranslated. The Arabic *Niyyah* is the feminine duel form of *Niyyahtayn*, not the male plural that's normally assigned to it.

There are some familiar elements of the story that make regular appearances throughout the *Nights*– among them, the desire of a common man to marry a princess, the unworldly power of the afreet (powerful jinn or demons), and the discovery of great treasures.

The story picks up on the fortunes of the two travellers at different points in time. Abou Neeut is always helped out of a tight spot, but he is diligent to seize the opportunities that open up to him—whether in building up his business, or in being a fair judge in the sultan's court.

Abou Neeuten, meanwhile, shows some willingness to work at being a merchant, but is soon distracted by the promise of what he assumes will be a life of greater adventure and wealth. He is of the untrustworthy, greedy type who pursue their own route to riches or fame without regard for others, but who ultimately fail to find wholeness.

Both men experience being in the dark well—Abou Neeuten descending there of his own volition, greedy for knowledge that will allow him to enjoy a similar life to Abou Neeut. But his jealous scheming leads to his own destruction. Abou Neeut is left to die, but is the one who is brought out into the light of day to meet a generous group of travellers, and then good fortune after arriving in Mosul.

There is an echo of the biblical story of Joseph and his brothers in the story. The experience of Abou Neeut—both as a respected merchant, and later as the closest adviser to the sultan—mirrors that of Joseph, whose brothers cannot recognise him when he is adorned in the fine clothes of high office.

Perhaps the brothers–like Abou Neeuten–are too focused on self-preservation to acknowledge the generosity of their host–blind, as it were, to being able to properly relate to the person who holds out a hand of friendship to them. So far gone are they along the path of self-destruction to be capable of meeting the one who has rescued them heart-to-heart.

The tale appears in Jonathon Scott's translation of the *Supplemental Nights, Volume 4*. Its conclusion frames another story of envy that's developed in the *Nights*, concerning the jealousy of the two elder sisters of Abou Neeut's wife. While Abou Neeut ultimately becomes sultan, we are not yet told that his and his queen's story will be one that continues "happily ever after". In fact, faith and good intention do again play a part in bringing about happiness for Abou Neeut, but that's a story to be told at another time.

Sinbad the Porter and the fourth voyage of Sinbad the Sailor

I have before related some of the strange tales that were told to me by Sinbad the Sailor–a rich man of Baghdad, whose company I had shared for each of the three nights before the story that I'm about to tell.

This man dwells in the most ostentatious luxury, but for a reason that is yet unclear to me, saw fit to allow me to sup with him, as well as offering me a gift of silver coins each time I have been given his audience.

I am Sinbad the Porter, a poor man whose dwelling place is the gutter and whose common sustenance is the leftover morsels of other men, which have been thrown out onto the street for the attention of the birds.

It is such in this unjust world that one man can live in such poverty, while others like my boastful host possess more than any man might ever need.

Still, I have been richly entertained these past nights, and my belly has welcomed the sumptuous foods that have been offered to me. So I again ventured to the table of my extravagant namesake last night, and here I recount to you the astonishing story that he shared with me. These are his very words as best I can recall them.

"I had not long returned to Baghdad following my third voyage, when a group of merchants came to the city, telling of their adventures and encounters with foreign peoples and exotic lands. My passion to journey was once more quickly aroused, and so I proposed to make a journey with them, carrying with us rich provisions from the treasures that I'd previously acquired.

We journeyed first to Basra, and from there set sail for many islands and far-off shores. We traded well, and wondered at the sights that greeted us. But one night, our ship was caught in the midst of a frightful tempest.

The ferocious gale forced us far from our course, and, fearing that our lives were in peril, our captain gave instruction for us to drop anchor. Thus secured, we hoped that we might be able to regain our path once the fierce winds receded.

Our anchorage did not hold. The winds ripped the ship's sails to shreds, even cutting through the very top of the cable that had tethered us to the sea's bed.

Suddenly, a wave of a height that we had never seen before came upon us. The ship rocked violently, and unable to steady ourselves, I and several of the crew were thrown from the deck into the angry, dark waters.

I cried out to Allah for my salvation, and–all praise to Him!–a large plank of wood drifted by me, which I was able to clamber upon. Several of my companions soon joined me on this makeshift raft, and we did our best to paddle, managing to stay afloat.

For two nights we wrestled against the angry sea, before the winds eventually subsided. Having given up nearly all hope of rescue, we were again spared when our tiny raft came to rest on the beach of a beautiful island. Here, we were able to gather herbs and other plants for our nourishment.

Having rested and recovered a little, we proceeded to explore the island's interior. We soon came upon what we supposed to be a house. No sooner had we arrived at its threshold than a group of men appeared around us. Without speaking a word, they indicated for us to follow them.

The natives presented us to whom we assumed to be their king, who ordered his servants to make a healthy feast for us. My companions eagerly consumed what they were given, drinking freely from the coconut oil that was made available in generous quantity.

I held back from accepting this apparent hospitality, suspecting a trick. And so it was that the others from my crew quickly became delirious, acting like madmen—becoming slaves to the natives' bidding.

We were treated to this unwholesome diet for many days, but I continued to resist taking from what was put before us. In a short time, my companions grew fat, but they stayed ignorant of their situation.

True to my suspicion, the natives proved to be cannibals. When one of our number grew sufficiently fat for the king's liking, the savages roasted him, before picking off his bones and devouring his raw flesh.

Because of my weak constitution, I was able to avoid the natives' attention for a time, but increasingly feared for my life. I thus resolved to escape from the enclosure where we were being held—a place not unlike a paddock where grazing animals might be put.

One night I let slip from the field, managing to escape the notice of the guard, whom I assumed the savages would call a herdsman. I hurried into the forest, not stopping until I was certain that I was far away from the natives' lair.

Finding at last pure spring water that I could drink, and feeding myself with the herbs that I was able to gather from the forest floor, I regained my strength by degrees. Resting in whatever sheltered places I could find by day, and journeying by night, I ventured seven days before eventually catching sight of men working in the distance, whom I assumed to be merchants.

I made quickly toward them, and was graciously received by their company. When I related my story to them, they confirmed that the place was well known for being a home of savages, who would devour anyone who came into their way.

The men treated me kindly, inviting me to share their food and wine, and entreating me to join their company. They brought me in time to their own land. Here, I was received warmly by their king and his court, who were astounded by the stories that I related.

I quickly made friends in this delightful place. The city's souks were alive with colour, their air filled with the sweet smells of the choicest spices and richest fruits. The centre was elegantly laid out, graced by many fine buildings and enlivened by charming gardens and playful fountains. I gave thanks to Allah for bringing me to such a place.

As in Baghdad, there were many horses in the city. However, I could not fail to notice that none were attired with saddles, nor with stirrups, nor bridles that might guide them. I therefore sought an audience with the king, to offer that I might attempt to make him such as these.

The king had never heard of such things, but I assured him that they would offer him a more comfortable ride, as well as affording greater agility and control.

Consequently, I commissioned a carpenter to make a saddletree, showing him the design that I had in mind. When this was completed, I filled the structure with wool, then covered it with felt and leather. I then attached leather straps to it, onto which stirrups might be fastened. These I charged a blacksmith to fashion, who took instruction from my design.

So too, the blacksmith forged a bit of a kind that I described, to which I attached a bridle, decorated with colourful silks and elegantly knit leather, as I thought befitting for a horse of the king's cavalry.

The king was delighted with my gift, and soon his chief vizier desired that I might similarly equip his own thoroughbred. Together with the carpenter and the blacksmith–to whom I taught the skill–I was soon overwhelmed with orders for saddles and bridles. Through this trade, I earned considerable riches and a fond reputation in the kingdom.

After some months, the king requested to see me to put forward a proposal that he was considering. He said that he was minded to marry me to a rich and high-ranking noblewoman. If my honour allowed, I should marry her forthwith and give up my plan to return to my homeland.

Feeling safe and happy in this place and sure that Allah had brought me here for His great purpose, I joyously accepted the king's offer, and was soon married to the most charming of women. We dwelt happily together for some years. However, no man can know the destiny that is appointed for him.

After a while, it happened that a neighbour of mine was overcome with grief, for his dear wife had just died. I tried to console this poor man, assuring him that–if Allah desired–he would soon find himself another wife, and that his days would surely be long in number.

"This cannot be so," lamented the man, "For it is the custom in our country to bury a man with his wife should she take leave before him, and likewise a wife with her husband, should he first give up the ghost."

I was astonished to hear of this vile custom, but my protesting was in vain. The following day, the townsfolk came and carried the poor man's wife on a brier, and led my neighbour with them to a place outside of the city.

There, on a slope of a mountain, they drew back a large stone—revealing the pit into which the couple were to be interred. The dead woman was lowered into the grave first, and then her husband was let down with the support of a rope of palm branches. He carried with him a flask of water and seven cakes of bread, which I assumed would offer him sustenance for no more than a few days.

Once the man had descended into the pit and loosened himself from the rope, the townsfolk covered the opening to the pit with the stone, then returned to the city.

Terrified at what I saw, I once more sought an audience with the king, to seek his counsel on whether foreigners who dwelt in the land would be subject to the same fate should their partner expire before them. The king told me that this was so, since it was believed that the souls of two lovers should never be parted.

I was greatly troubled after hearing his advice, fearing that I would suffer a terrible death were my dear wife to die before me. After a time, however, I contented myself that she was in fine health, and that it was most likely that I would meet my maker long before her.

I diverted my attention for a while, but it was not long before my wife fell sick. Within a few days, a terrible fever took hold of her, and within a short time, she died.

My grieving for my wife was quite natural, but my grieving for myself was more than any person should have to bear. Soon enough, the townsfolk came to carry my wife on a brier to her mountain grave, leading me behind her.

My protest that the custom of burying two lovers together should not apply to a settler in their land fell on deaf ears. After they had lowered my wife's body into the pit, they forced me to follow on behind her, cutting loose the rope of palm branches when I refused to let go of this. Together with my seven cakes of bread and a flask of water, I was left alone in the cavern to die.

I berated myself, convinced that it was due to my own misdeeds that I found myself in this terrible place. I thought that it would be better had I perished at sea, or felt the blow of a sword's steel, than to wait for hunger and thirst to take their toll.

"Mighty Allah, I have failed You!" I cried. "You alone have the power to save me!"

At first, I sat amid the decaying bones of the many bodies that had been let down into the pit. The stench was most powerful—acrid and unavoidable.

After a while, I began to explore the cavern, which I discovered was much larger than I'd originally supposed. I rested in a corner of the dark space, drinking sparingly from my flask, and taking only a small quantity of my bread with each bite, hoping that I might prolong my sustenance.

After what I imagine may have been several days–though in that dark place, I could not determine what was night and what was day–I was startled by a blinding light, streaming into the darkness from the cavern's ceiling. Adjusting my eyes, I realised that the holding stone had been rolled away, and presently the dead body of a man was lowered into the pit.

This was followed by the loud wailing and screaming of a woman, whom I assumed to be his wife. Like many before her, she was lowered into the grave by means of the rope.

She had not seen me and, seizing the moment, I smote her with the thighbone of a man that I found beside me. I struck her several times, until I was certain that life had escaped her. I reasoned that my swift action made for a kinder death for her, than were she to die slowly from hunger and thirst. The cakes of bread and flask of water that she brought would at the same time sustain my own life a little more–I reasoned that it is better that one survives for a while, than two die in agony.

Others followed on after her, to whom I dealt further blows. In this manner, I was able to sustain my life, though I was no wiser about devising a plan for my salvation.

I continued to pray to Allah, pleading with Him to offer me a respite. It happened that after a time, I was disturbed by a rustling noise coming from one of the corners of the cavern. Upon investigation, I discovered that the sound was caused by some rodent or other creature, which had burrowed its way into the mountain cave along a shallow tunnel. As best I could, I followed the beast as it scurried away.

At times, a small beam of light came into view in the distance, disappearing and reappearing as I navigated the tunnel's uneven surface. Soon the light grew in intensity, and I then discovered that it showed the way to a crevice in the mountain.

I was able to manoeuvre my body through the narrow opening, and then found myself standing on the exposed side of the mountain, which sloped steeply toward the sea below.

I assumed that animals had widened the opening after discovering a way to enter the cavern, where they might feed on the human bones and decaying skin. The steep climb of the mountain above me suggested that its slopes were inaccessible and probably unknown to the people of the city that dwelt on the other side.

I praised Allah for bringing me to this place, and resolved to spend my daylight hours there, lest I espy a passing ship. I set about making panniers, using materials salvaged from some of the vestments of the deceased, then filled these with the jewels and gold that adorned many of the dead bodies. When newcomers were brought into the pit, I killed them—both to foreshorten their suffering, and to provide for my continued sustenance.

One day, while I was standing on the cliff, I observed a ship that was making speed on the horizon. Quickly, I attached a shawl that I had brought with me to a large staff. I began waving my makeshift flag excitedly, hoping that the seafarers might catch sight of it.

With the grace of Allah, my distress signal was at last noticed, and a small boat was sent to collect me. The men who ventured to rescue me demanded to hear my story, being astonished that any man could survive in such an inhospitable place. They carried me to their ship, together with my panniers that were filled with jewels, and there I was presented to their captain.

"Pray tell me how you came to be in such a place as this? Never in my many travels in these waters have I observed humans living on these cliffs," he petitioned me.

I repeated my story, explaining how I had come to be shipwrecked and had been washed ashore on the island after clinging to a makeshift raft, made from the windswept remains of the vessel.

However, I did not relate the detail of how I had sustained myself in the cavern, fearing that there might be kinsfolk of the islanders among the crew.

Grateful for my salvation, I pleaded with the captain to take from the jewels that I had gathered, but he refused.

"We treat all whom we rescue kindly, giving thanks to God," he replied. "If a man is in need of clothing, we fetch this for him. When we dock at a favourable port, we offer a gift of money to help him find his way back to prosperity."

We sailed for a time from island to island and from port to port, before finally coming to the great city of Basra. Here, I bided my time for a while, before returning to Baghdad, where I was warmly received by my family.

I gave thanks to Allah for bringing me safely home, gave alms to the poor, clothed the naked, and fed the hungry. Then I returned to my life of merriment— though I would suffer with great shaking and fear whenever I recalled my entombment in the cavern."

Here, the sailor finished the tale of his fourth voyage. He promised to entertain me again the following evening with a story of a yet further treacherous voyage.

Sinbad the Porter retired to his bed, taking the gift of one hundred dirham that his host had presented to him. There, he spent the night full of joy and excitement, marvelling at what the wealthy adventurer had told him.

Baghdad Hilton

My name is Akram Al-Rashedi. I have lived in Baghdad for all of my forty-five years, excepting the time that I served in the army. I fought in Kuwait in 1991, and later was sent to the east of our country, where I was forced to fight against my fellow Shia brothers in the marshy floodplain of the Euphrates.

I have faced death on a daily basis throughout most of my lifetime. Whether in war–praying that I do not fall victim to a suicide bombing–or battling against starvation, mine hasn't been an easy ride. There's nothing particularly unusual about this–around here, the sound of mortar attacks and explosives being detonated is so commonplace, that most of us let the thunderous noise pass over us as though it were the distant rumble of traffic.

The city wasn't always like this. My mother used to tell me what life was like back in her youth. Then, Baghdad was one of the greatest cities in the world. "It was idyllic," she used to recall. "The elegant buildings, the shining domes and towering minarets of the mosques, children playing in the parks that lined the Tigris, old men sipping arak in the coffee bars...Life was peaceful then, and we hoped for a brilliant future.

"People would come from all over the world to visit sacred shrines and marvel at priceless artworks, to barter with the colourful souls who peddled their magnificently patterned carpets and ornate goldwork in the busy souks. Here, they could find magnificent palaces, quays bustling with boats unloading their cargos, and beautifully manicured lawns".

I suppose that this is the way it should have been for a city that was once at the heart of the Muslim world. Baghdad was a crossroads for traders from East and West, on the cusp of recognising great oil wealth, and a mecca for travellers, diplomats, and anyone who loved living the high life.

Our house was small, but adequate. My father was a teacher, and was well regarded in our community. We never lacked for food, and my parents never worried about letting me play on the streets–even late into the night. That was back in the 1970's–still a difficult time–but never as difficult as the years that were to follow.

Now I live in Teneke Village, a rambling slum of discarded oil cans and other assorted junk on the edge of Sadr City. I, like most of the folk who live here, have used the cans to build a makeshift shelter for myself, as well as making a little cash by collecting and selling some of them as scrap metal. This barely earns me enough to pay for a cup of rice each day, but somehow I have survived–which is more than I can say for many of my old childhood chums and army comrades.

They are not the only ones who've gone–to my shame, I played a part in my own father's demise. I didn't realise what I was doing at the time, being only seven years old. No one had told me that idle chatter in the playground could be dangerous.

My father hated Saddam, who treated us Shiites especially harshly. Many of my tribe were beaten up or taken away. Some we never saw again. My father's job was always under threat, and he had to swear allegiance to our leader.

Publicly, my father was a model citizen. He played deference to the Ba'ath Party, and avoided any protests that might draw unwelcome attention.

Privately, he hated the life that he'd come to know. Like my mother, he often recalled "the good old days". Now I understand how right he was to recognize that long-ago time as being a golden era.

At times, the pressures of his work caused my father to erupt into a rage within the confines of our home, where he felt safe to express himself.

"They're forcing us to fix the marks of kids whose parents are members of the Ba'ath Party!" I remember him screaming one evening. "Not even the past is respected any more...they're making us rewrite history to blank out all the good things that our country achieved before Saddam!" he protested on another.

He had many words to describe Saddam and his tyrannical family. As a seven-year-old, I didn't appreciate the meaning of such terms at the time. And so I thought nothing wrong when our teacher asked us in class one day to suggest some names that we might use to describe our beloved leader. I simply repeated what I had heard my father say–"bully", "thug", "murderer", and the like.

My teacher was keen to know where I'd learned such words, and I saw no reason to avoid telling her the truth. My classmates seemed terrified that I'd been so candid.

My father was led away from his own classroom several days later. We never saw him again, nor did we ever learn where he was taken. Only through my own experience many years later–which I will tell you about in due course–did I learn about the horrors that awaited those who dared to criticize the President.

My mother beat me implacably when I told her what I'd revealed in class. Every part of my body felt the weight of her hand, and that was beside the shoes, and the jars, and the apples that she aimed at me.

She wept for days without stopping. Often, I thought that she was ready to throw herself into the muddy swells of the Tigris. But when she was finally able to look at me without shouting, I think she realised that I'd intended no harm. How could any anyone have wished for their father to be dragged away to face Saddam's dogs?

"You have ruined our lives!" she wailed, "But you're my son, and you don't know what you did". Finally, she hugged me and assured me of her love. Then she made me promise that I would never say anything bad about the regime again—whatever she or I might really believe.

I did my best to stay out of trouble after then. I carried out all the errands that my mother asked me to, and I was careful not to criticise anyone or anything. At least, I managed to keep my profile low for more than twenty years.

When I finished my schooling, I enlisted in the army. I hated being away from my mother, and detested the brutal physical regime that my training involved. But I was commended by my Corporal, who told me that I was a good example of what an Iraqi soldier should be.

When we were sent to Kuwait to take back the territory that had once been under the authority of Basra, my section was full of excitement and pride after relieving the Kuwaitis of their hated ruler, and bringing this jewel of the Gulf back into Iraqi control. However, our jubilation wasn't to last long. When the United States-led coalition attacked, even our massive army was no match for the force that was let loose on us.

Many of my companions simply fled their positions, traumatised by the brilliant explosion of firepower that continually bombarded us. Despite being in grave danger, I held my position. Through my perseverance, I was later to save my sanity—for among those who ran in terror from the battlefield, many were later shot for desertion, or had their ears cut off for not obeying orders.

I served in the army for a total of twelve years, reaching the rank of Staff Sergeant. When I demobbed and returned to Baghdad, I was unsure what profession I might take up, not having had an opportunity to gain experience with a trade. My first priority was to nurse my mother, who had been diagnosed with lung cancer.

The neighbourhood where I'd grown up had been much changed by the war over Kuwait, even though nearly ten years had passed since that terrible event. Many roads were still pitted with potholes, whole blocks were littered with rubble where houses once stood, and even where half a wall remained, nothing stood behind.

Miraculously, my mother's flat was one of the few that avoided being struck. My tough old mother had battled against starvation, worried constantly about my safety on the front-line, and of course never overcame the trauma of losing my father.

Unfortunately, lung cancer was one battle that she couldn't come through. This awful disease ate into her body but never weakened her spirit. I cared for her for six months, before she finally succumbed and gave up the ghost.

After my mother died, I set up as a book trader, working a stall in al-Muttanabi Street–a lively place in one the oldest quarters of the city. While my business was never destined to make me rich, I earned enough to pay my way, and I enjoyed the banter that I shared with regular customers.

From time to time, conversation turned to the news stories of the day. Few people openly gave opinions on the affairs of the President or his family, nor about the decisions that were decreed from the Republican Palace. But subjects such as the fortunes of our national football team, or the state of affairs in the north of our country, were fair game for discussion.

My father's disappearance was always raw in my consciousness, and I was always wary about appearing to be even slightly critical of the dealings of the Ba'ath

Party and its leader. Too many people had met gruesome ends for even hinting at dissension.

One thing that did kindle my anger was what I saw as the unfair disparity between the lives of the rich and ordinary people of our city. Saddam and his entourage lived in palatial luxury, wanting for nothing. Somehow, despite the severe sanctions that had been imposed on our country, the elite filled their cellars with expensive wines smuggled out of Europe, lounged around their large swimming pools, and sported the latest Patek Philippe and Rolex watches that they'd snapped up on their private-jet escapades to Paris and Geneva.

It's said that Uday, the eldest of Saddam's precious sons, attended lavish parties virtually every night–that's if he wasn't tearing around town in one of the many Lamborghinis that he'd looted from Kuwait, or hanging around with some hapless model that he'd picked up at one of his clubs.

One morning, the newspaper reported that Saddam was planning to build a new outrageous palace, adding to the eighty or so that he already owned. This abuse caused me to temporarily lose my senses.

"How can he squander money on another unnecessary folly when so many people are starving?" I demanded, hoping to attract a sympathetic response from one of my regular customers who was conversing with me at my stall.

"That family. Nothing–not even all the riches that were possessed by the great Caliph al-Mansour–will be enough for them!"

My customer smiled discretely, as if to acknowledge his agreement, but quickly moved the conversation onto other concerns–matters that were less likely to attract the attention of passers-by.

I wish now that I'd followed his example. Ba'ath Party spies were everywhere, and a busy marketplace in the centre of Baghdad was not the smartest place to strike up a conversation about the unfairness of my lot.

After finishing my business for the day, I packed away my stall and loaded my books onto my handcart. Starting away from the market, I suddenly felt someone's hand pressing down firmly on my shoulder. "Akram Al-Rashedi, you are to come with us!" came a voice.

Briefly glancing over my shoulder, I saw two burly men behind me, dressed in business suits and jet black glass spectacles. I found each of my arms being gripped from behind, and in an instant, a leather strap was fastened around my wrists. The men led me to a BMW SUV that was parked close to the souk, and I was swiftly bundled into its boot.

We sped through the city–I think crossing the Tigris, but I couldn't be sure. The car raced over potholes and assorted obstacles, never seeming to stop for other traffic. After a time, the bumps and turns that were throwing me around in the back came to an end. The car slowed, stopped briefly at several points, and then traversed a perfectly smooth road surface. I wondered whether we had entered the presidential compound. Later, I was to learn that this was indeed our destination.

When the car came to rest, the men escorted me from the boot. They manhandled me more abruptly than before, and I'm sure would have dragged me along the ground had I attempted to resist their leading. I pleaded to know what was happening to me, but the men carried on with their business without even acknowledging that I'd spoken.

We went inside a utilitarian, grey-stone building, which looked from the outside like any anonymous office block. I was led down several flights of steps, and then along a poorly-lit corridor. Stopping about half way along, my clothes were stripped from me, including my underwear. A weighty steel door on one side of the corridor was swung open, and then, grabbing my hair, one of the men thrust me into what was to become a place of nightmares.

The force of the throw caused me to knock my head on the opposing wall, but the shock that this brought was quickly overtaken by the sting of a strike across my back, accompanied by the force of a kick to the back of my left calf.

My captors left me alone following this welcome, after directing a torrent of spittle at the back of my head, and yelling as they slammed the door–"Welcome to the Baghdad Hilton!".

The door took up most of the area on one side of my cell. Perfectly square, I was unable to fully lie down in the puny space, and even when crouching in a corner, had no room to fully stretch out my legs. Save for the bare light bulb–which was never switched off–the entire room was painted blood-red. Even the back of the door, the floor and the ceiling were painted in the same manner. My hosts had generously left a blanket that I could wrap around myself, but I was soon to discover a more pressing need for this.

I waited for what seemed like many hours before I was visited again. A small grille at the base of the door was opened, allowing a small bowl of rice and a beaker of water to be passed through to me. This was to be my daily diet from that moment on.

I soon learned that my cries to be allowed an escort to visit the toilet were in vain. My cell was to be my toilet, as well as being my dining place and my bedroom. As my soon uncontrollable deposits of body waste increased, I reserved use of my blanket to conceal the mess, while the thin covering also provided a little protection against the disgusting stench.

Often, I would hear screaming from further down the corridor, or some distant room. I heard other sounds too, such as the piercing whine of an electric drill, or the loud rip of a chainsaw. I reasoned that if they were prepared to feed human beings to Saddam's dogs, then no act of evil that the imagination could conceive would be beyond the wit of the monsters that ran this place.

The long periods between receiving my rice and water marked out what I assume were whole days, but to be honest, in that hellhole I quickly lost all sense of what was night and day.

Curiously, I was left alone for what seemed like many days. The terrible screams and infernal sounds continued, and of course preoccupied my mind. I was certain that it wouldn't be long before I faced my own appointment with the torture specialists. That is if crouching in a tiny, stinking, blood-washed hole isn't enough to break anyone.

Eventually, without warning, my door was swung open. The two men that had brought me here were waiting outside. One took a grip on my hair, yanking me out into the corridor. The other then brutally seized my arm, forcing me to follow him into a room at the end of the corridor. There, I was greeted by a uniformed man, who sat behind a table.

Two thugs stood either side of the seated man, while my familiar escorts stood at my rear. The man whom I assumed to be my interrogator passed a derisory comment on the size of my genitals, causing the others to break into a hearty chuckle. He then proceeded to tell me why I had aroused the interest of Saddam's Security Service. I quickly learned that my unguarded comments in the marketplace had been overheard by an operative, and that my entire biography had been thoroughly researched.

"Most people who complain about the generous provisions of our gracious leader don't leave this place without losing a limb or two," he nonchalantly went on. "We see that you have a good service record, and that you didn't abandon your post in Kuwait. In very exceptional circumstances, you are fortunate to receive the very lightest of punishments, subject to your understanding that you will be hanged if you are ever again found to discredit our supreme leader or his family. You will receive one hundred lashes, five to be administered over each of the next twenty weeks."

In a state of complete disbelief and for reasons that now betray me, I thanked and saluted my adjudicator, whoever he may have been. I was led back to my cell, where I remained for the duration of my sentence.

My beatings were harsh, hurting me as much psychologically as they did physically. Still, I continued to hope that the judgement I'd received would be the end of my suffering. So it was, after my final trip down the corridor to the large room where I endured my flogging, that I was dressed, blindfolded, bundled into the boot of a car, and driven away from the compound.

After a time, the car stopped, and I heard its doors being slammed. The thugs dragged me out of the boot, then threw me into a dry ditch at the roadside. After I heard the car speed away, I managed to free myself from the leather strap, which this time was quite loosely tied around my wrists.

I could hardly believe my good fortune—against all the odds, I had escaped the prison from which very few returned. I kept my face pinned to the ground for a long time, although I was desperate for water. My military training had taught me to assess my situation before immediately giving in to my body's needs. I knew that if I exposed my eyes to the sunlight too quickly, I could easily be blinded. The dim, blood-red impression of my cell would likely stay with me for a long time.

After some time, I gradually lifted my head, and still shielding my eyes with my hands, slowly allowed them to open. I then brought my face back to the ground, before repeating this motion. I continued with this practice for sometime, each time allowing my eyes a little longer to absorb whatever light they could. Eventually, I felt ready to face the onslaught of brightness, took off my blindfold and lifted myself out of the trench. I found myself lying on the outskirts of Sadr City, not far from where I live today.

I returned home, where I rested for some days. In the weeks that followed, I recovered my strength by degrees, and then again began my business of selling books.

I was very aware that it was likely that I was being watched–and knowing the fate that awaited me should I utter anything that might be considered to be critical of the regime–I kept my conversation to a minimum.

A terrible new war was soon to rain destruction on the city. This time, the Americans and their allies were not going to stop until Saddam himself had fallen. I was recalled into the army, and was quickly dispatched to aid the resistance against the invasion.

For almost three weeks, a spectacular fireworks show illuminated the Baghdad skyline. Highly sophisticated weapons pummelled the palatial compound. Rumours began to spread that members of Saddam's Cabinet had begun to disperse, having conceded that this was one conflict that they couldn't win. Still, Saddam continued to send his Information Officer on daily missions to report on the invincibility of our forces to the Western media. No one took this fantasy seriously.

The aerial bombardment ended quickly, and American troops took up residence in our city. For a brief time, there was celebration, especially when we learned that Saddam had been caught hiding in a spider-hole at a supposed safe house. His statues were toppled, and other physical symbols of the Ba'ath Party's power were destroyed.

I hoped for a better life following the overthrow of the regime, but–as had so often been the case in my life–my hope was in vain. A caretaker government came into power after the Americans passed back authority to Iraqis, but this proved to be incapable of re-establishing stability in our broken nation.

The city seemed to fracture into many pieces, as lawlessness ruled and tribal loyalties took hold of communities. Worse, insurgents flooded the city–some still loyal to the old regime, but mostly religious zealots who, like me, wanted an end to the foreigners' continued occupation.

I had been made homeless by the war–my house being destroyed by fire, which had claimed my stock of books in the process. I had since moved to the place where I am now, selling tin cans to buy rice, and sheltering among the rats and sewerage.

I could not try to sell books any more, even if I had the stock to start with. Few people spend their free time travelling between neighbourhoods now. The suicide bombings make unnecessary moving around too dangerous, while few people are ready to spend their meagre savings buying old books.

Curiously, my own fortunes have taken a turn in recent weeks. This has happened since a man that I at first didn't recognise came looking for me in the village. It turned out that he was Akram Al-Rashedi, someone who not only shared my name, but who'd been a classmate of mine at my first school.

I didn't recognize Akram at first. Our paths hadn't crossed for many years. What's more, I wasn't accustomed to being approached by such a smartly dressed businessman.

It turned out that Akram was a senior executive for the South Oil Company. He'd worked abroad for most of his career, gaining experience with other oil multinationals. This had made him rich by Western standards, and when he returned to Baghdad, he had built an expensive villa, some miles to the west of the city.

For reasons that weren't at all clear to me, Akram was keen to entertain me at his miniature palace. He drove me across town in his immaculately polished Mercedes, and treated me to a diet of expensive meats and fresh vegetables.

During our meal, he related tales of his adventures to me. It seems that he hadn't always been satisfied spending his life in luxury apartments and plush offices, and had often volunteered to head up explorations searching for new oil fields. This had taken him to many parts of the world. He claimed that his life had often been in danger, that he'd had to negotiate his escape from drug barons and corrupt oil officials, whose power bases his projects threatened to disrupt.

I was struck with wonder by his stories, which portrayed a life so different from my own. When I was brought back to my village, I examined my own lot, considering how unfair it was that some people could live in such luxury, while others like me fought day-to-day against starvation.

Still, I welcomed the interruption to my merciless grind. Akram invited me to join him again the following week, and so too the week following that. Yesterday, I was entertained a fourth time, but on this occasion, he revealed something that has left me thunderstruck.

"My dear Akram," he began, as he filled my glass with wine. "I have quite a confession to make to you. I pray that you will hear my full story, and will not hold a vengeance against me."

He continued to recount some of the adventures that we had enjoyed at school. I did not then know him as a friend, but we had shared many common experiences.

"I remember the day when we were asked to suggest words to describe the President," he continued. "Like everyone in the class, I was astonished at what you said. When I went home, I asked my father what those words meant. Of course, he was anxious to know where I had heard them, and so I related the story of what had happened in class."

On hearing his admission, I slammed my wine glass back onto the table, causing its blood-red liquid to spill over the pure white tablecloth that was laid across it. I felt deep anger brewing in my stomach, but I kept my composure, resisting an outburst or taking an action that I might later regret.

Akram continued: "Perhaps like you, I didn't appreciate the importance of what I was saying. I later learned that your father had been taken away, and I'm sure that my own father was responsible for this. He was a loyal member of the Ba'ath Party, and a great admirer of Saddam."

I brought my glass to my mouth in a pretence of acting normally, but had lost all appetite for my wine. I stared at Akram for some time, trying to gain a measure of the man. I slowly concluded that his crime was no different to my own—we were both seven-year-olds, ignorant of what we were saying.

After a time Akram went on: "You know that we parted company when our schooldays came to an end. I was sent to the University of Baghdad, and then started in my first position in the oil business. I made good progress in the company, and was rewarded with a role that involved circumventing the sanctions that we faced after the Kuwait fiasco.

My job involved secretly selling oil to our neighbours at a discount, who then sold it on to the world market at standard price. We still made 80% of the going rate, while our neighbours were pocketing the rest for virtually no effort at all."

I listened incredulously as Akram continued his story. "I happened to be in al-Muttanabi Street on the day that the Secret Service picked you up, recognising you as the one whose father I had inadvertently shopped. I've never forgotten that terrible incident, nor forgiven myself for my part in it.

"Because my work involved occasionally liaising with agents of the regime, I was able to find out where you were being held, and then was able to intervene on your behalf. There was a custom of going lightly on the family or friends of respected party members who'd been picked up for questioning, and so my suggestion that you should be spared with a slap on the wrist was taken on board."

I was tempted to complain that spending six months in a toilet and suffering the violence of one hundred lashes was more than a "slap on the wrist", but I realised that this was not of Akram's doing.

"Few people come out of that place alive," he continued. "Most eventually confess to whatever the bullies want them to say, but still end up losing a hand, or an eye, or having the life squeezed out of them at the end of a rope. I'm so sorry for what you suffered, for what happened to your father."

I could see that Akram was speaking honestly. It was now clear to me why he'd been so keen to discover where I was living, and to want to make amends for the past.

"Everything I have is not worth anything if I can't be true to myself," he went on. "This I have learned only recently. I feel quite a kinship with you, even though our paths have been set so far apart. My friend–and I hope that I can honour you with that title–I want to offer you a bed to stay here in my house. You will have your own apartment, and I will make sure that you never go hungry again. Perhaps you'll want to reflect on my offer, but I would like you to be sure that it will give me great pleasure if you feel ready to accept it."

"My friend," I replied. "I need no time to consider your proposal. I see that our actions in our childhood are no different from each other. Your company enlivens my soul, and I too feel a strong bond with you. It will give me great pleasure to share your company and your home."

This was an easy decision to make. Had I doubted Akram's sincerity, I would rather have continued my life among the oil cans of Teneke Village. But in a few short weeks, Akram and I had grown to be more than friends. On this last night that I spend in the sewer, I feel at last that I'm starting off on a better future.

Afterword

The fourth voyage of Sinbad the Sailor is reckoned by some to be the most gruesome of the series. Peter D.

Molan suggests that this middle tale of the seven represents a turning point in the nature of the disasters that the adventurer encounters[10].

These rise in their intensity over the course of the three preceding tales, then correspondingly reduce in the stories that follow.

As the terrors recounted by the sailor increase, so does the fascination and enjoyment of the porter. At the end of the fourth tale, for example, we are told that he spent the night full of joy, not ruing what he perceives as being the injustice of his poverty.

The full cycle of stories about the sailor's adventures ultimately reveal that his hospitality toward the porter is really an attempt to resolve his guilt. Not only has he accumulated far greater riches than any person might ever need, but at times he has done so through devious and devilish means.

There is a hint of his awareness of this in the fourth tale. Notably, the sailor doesn't reveal to the crew that rescues him that his survival regime on the island involved killing the innocent people who were let down into the pit. He steals from their provisions, and robs them of their jewels.

---

[10] Peter D. Molan, *Sinbad the Sailor, a commentary on the ethics of violence*, in Marzolph (ed.) (2006), *Arabian Nights Reader*, pp 327-346.

Always, the sailor's telling of his story attempts to justify his actions—in the case of striking down the partners of the dead, by claiming that this curtailed their suffering, while permitting at least one life (his own) to be sustained.

A romantic and a fantasist he may be, but the sailor's generosity toward the porter can't be explained by unselfish giving alone. By giving alms and receiving the porter into his home, Sinbad the Sailor attempts to make amends with his God.

The two Sinbads are really one and the same person—a matter that is made clear by the fact that they both share the same name. One is the alter ego of the other—the shadow self that challenges and exposes the weaknesses of its opposite.

To achieve healthy and wholesome development, both natures must ultimately be reconciled. In this tale, both "Sinbads" are now fully engaged in a dialogue, and if they are both able to learn from each other, this bodes well for their ultimate coming together.

As Sinbad the Sailor increasingly realises that he cannot justify his bad actions with the poor excuses that he's created to satisfy himself, so Scheherazade—the story's real narrator—might have hoped to prompt King Shahryah to see that his own justification for continuing to slaughter the women who entertain him does not really hold water.

To a greater or lesser extent, most of us might prefer to convince ourselves that we are without fault for leading the lifestyles that we do—for example, by being sparing in sharing the riches that we've earned, leaving caring for the needy to others, and seeking to defend the organisations, neighbourhoods, and assumed rights that we believe we're entitled to.

It might be easy to frame the Sinbad stories as nothing more than wildly imaginative tale-telling, but to do so would be to miss the salutary lesson that the storyteller probably intended.

The story of the barber's fifth brother

When my father died, he left an equal share of his estate to my six brothers and I. Each of us received one hundred dirhams, which we could choose to spend as we best thought would profit us.

I will now tell you the tale of my fifth brother, Alnaschar, who was among the laziest men in our town. This brother of mine was satisfied to while away his time begging for money, contenting himself with what he received. Never before had he been given so much money as that gifted him by our father, and he was greatly perplexed about how he should invest his inheritance.

Eventually, he spent the whole one hundred dirhams on a piece of glassware, which he obtained at a wholesale price. He positioned the glass before his sitting place on the street, waiting to catch the eye of a passer-by who might consent to buy it. As he did so, he spoke aloud his plan, which he had meditated and ruminated on over many hours.

"From the sale of this crystal, I will earn two hundred dirhams," he began. "Buying two more similar pieces of glass, I will then sell these for the same profit—making me four hundred dirhams. With my earnings, I will buy four more crystal works, generating a certain income of eight hundred dirhams. Soon, I will have made more than one thousand dirhams for myself, and with this money, I shall then begin to trade in gold, diamonds, and pearls.

When I have accumulated still more wealth, I will buy a fine mansion, staffed by slaves and eunuchs, and surrounded by stables that will house the most elegantly formed horses. I will dress in a rich man's attire, and entertain myself with the music of famous musicians, while enjoying the delicate performances of the most exquisite dancers.

When I have accumulated one hundred thousand dirhams, I will send a message to the chief vizier, requesting that he marry his daughter to me. I have heard that she is of exceptional beauty, as well as being gifted in conversation, humour, and the arts.

With my petition, I will offer the vizier one thousand gold pieces, to be paid to him on the night of the marriage. Should he decline my request–which I consider to be most unlikely–I will bring his daughter to my house of my own accord, where she will consent to marry me.

Once we are married, I will buy my wife ten eunuchs, and I will attire myself like a prince, parading through the town on a horse adorned with a saddle of golden silk. My slaves will accompany me as I ride among the people–who will make way for my path, and show me the greatest respect.

When I arrive at the palace of the vizier, I will descend from my horse, and then be escorted through the grand atrium by my entourage, where the vizier shall graciously receive me. One of my slaves shall hand the vizier a purse, which will be filled with one thousand gold pieces, and another shall do likewise–proving to the vizier that I am doubly true to my word.

Everyone will marvel at my generosity. Returning with great ceremony to my mansion, my wife will applaud me for my congenial meeting with her father. I will offer her a rich present. If she does likewise, I shall refuse her gift. I will not consent to her leaving her quarters without my permission. When I visit her, she will know that I demand her respect.

I will keep a high seat, and feign disinterest when she entreats me to caress her. I will not make any reply to her servants who beg me to be kind to her. They will prostrate themselves before me, but I shall ignore them.

Assuming that my wife is not sufficiently well attired and perfumed to be received by me, they will escort her away to tend to her hair and perfect her appearance. I too will change into a magnificent costume. When they return to me, I shall continue to disregard my wife, until they have at least entreated me as eagerly as they did before.

This I will do on the very first day of our marriage, such that my wife comes to know how she is to conduct herself for the rest of her days.

When the wedding festivities have ended, my wife will retire to bed before me. I will come and lay beside her, but keeping my back toward her. I will not speak to her, nor entertain her glance.

When morning comes, my wife will implore me to comfort her, but I shall continue to keep my distance. Then she will send for her mother, lamenting how she has failed me, and seeking her mother's help to petition me on her behalf.

Her mother will prostrate herself before me, begging that I show favour toward her daughter. She will hail me, and beseech me to look kindly on her offspring, but I will not humour her. Eventually, she will encourage her daughter to bring a glass of wine to me, reasoning that I may not be so hard of heart as to refuse an offering from such a fair hand.

"My master, my lord, my beloved!" my wife will cry, "Please accept this glass from your humble servant!"

I will refuse to take the glass, and keep my eyes from resting on her.

"My dear lord, I will not fail to wait for you to take this glass from me," my wife will continue, her voice trembling and her heart beating wildly.

At this, I will cast her a stern stare, and strike out at her with my foot."

My brother was so immersed in his fantasy, that he kicked out in front of him, as if imitating the punishment that he planned to deal to his wife. However, his precious glassware stood in front of him, and in an instant this was dashed to pieces.

Disturbed by the noise of the shattering glass, my brother came to his senses. He then rended his clothes and beat his hands on the pavement in despair.

"How foolish I have been! How vain and irresponsible! Now, because of my greediness, I have nothing!" he scolded himself, unable to stop himself from loud wailing.

As it was a Friday and approaching noontime, many people passed by where my brother sat, enquiring about his woes. One richly dressed woman, who was passing among them on a mule, sent her servant to enquire why my brother was so distressed. Hearing his story, she ordered her servant to hand a purse to him, containing whatever money she had to hand.

Overcome with great emotion, my brother prostrated himself before the woman, shouting praises to Allah. Retiring to his house, he discovered that the purse contained no fewer than five hundred dirhams.

Presently, an elderly woman knocked on the door of my brother's house, praying that she might make her ablutions there, before presenting herself at the mosque. My brother willingly received her, and after she had bowed to him and repeated her gratitude for his kindness, he took two gold coins from his purse, which he desired she take from him as an offering of alms.

"My dear man, this I will not do!" she returned, seeming to be affronted, "I am well provided for by a rich woman of this city, and should not be taken to be an impudent beggar!"

My brother was not sufficiently clever to appreciate the woman's intention–who had only refused to take the two coins from him in the hope that he might offer her more.

"Might you allow me the pleasure of being introduced to this fine lady?" my brother continued.

"With great joy!" the woman replied. "I am sure that she will desire to marry you, and then to put you in charge of all that she possesses. Gather your gold, and follow me."

Perceiving himself to be blessed with good fortune, my brother collected his five hundred dirhams, and proceeded to follow the woman. After a while, they came to a large house, where a slave received them at the gate.

My brother was invited to enter first, and was taken across a magnificently polished courtyard, and then into a hallway, which was arrayed with fine tapestries and sculptures. Here, my brother was asked to wait, while the woman went to speak to the one whom he was certain must be a very wealthy woman.

Presently, a young woman of exceptional beauty presented herself. She engaged my brother in pleasant conversation for a while, and then led him into another room, where she said that she must leave him for a moment.

The woman did not return, but in her place, sent a gargantuan slave, who was armed with a scimitar. Dealing a single blow to my brother's head, the slave then proceeded to rub salt into his wound, believing him to be dead. While still conscious, my brother was then dragged to lie over a trapdoor, although he pretended to be lifeless. The trapdoor was opened, and my brother fell sharply into a dark pit, where he observed the dead bodies of several other men.

My brother waited in this terrible place for two full days. Then, when the house fell silent and night provided some cover, he managed to release the trapdoor, then finding a place where he might hide himself.

The following morning, my brother saw the old woman leaving the house, presuming that she had gone in search of another victim. He waited for many minutes until he was sure that she would not see him, and then crept away from the house. He came quickly to my dwelling, where he told me all that had happened.

With the help of herbs and medicines, my brother's wound was healed by degrees. He then related to me his plan to avenge himself of the old woman. To prepare himself, he took a large bag–one large enough to hold five hundred pieces of gold. This he filled with broken glass.

My brother then took on the habit of an old woman, concealing a blade under his dress. Taking the bag of broken glass, he ventured into the souk, where he hoped to come across the old woman.

When at last he saw her, he approached her, and–affecting a woman's voice–enquired whether she knew where he might find someone who could loan him a pair of scales, such that he could weigh his bag of five hundred dirhams. He claimed that he had just brought this sum with him from Persia.

"My dear lady," the woman replied, "You could not have asked a better person! My brother possesses a pair of scales and will willingly weigh your purse for you, but we must hasten quickly to his house, before he sets off for his business."

My brother followed behind the woman, who soon brought him to the same house that she had led him to before. The slave who guarded the gate granted them access, and my brother was led to the same richly decorated hall that he'd been brought to before.

The old woman invited him to sit down, and then went to fetch her supposed brother, whom my brother immediately recognised as the giant slave who had earlier left him for dead. Without hesitation, my brother drew out the blade that was hidden beneath his clothes, and dealt the slave a fierce blow to the neck. In an instant, the grotesque slave's head was severed from his body.

Presently, the slave who was responsible for guarding the gate arrived with a cup of salt, expecting this to be administered to the newly arrived victim. However, my brother took swift revenge on him too— cutting off his head with a single blow.

After a time, the old woman returned, and was deeply troubled by what she saw.

"Do you not know who I am?" bellowed my brother, who had now removed his veil. The woman pleaded that she did not.

"I am the one who entertained you in my house, where you could perform your ablutions before prayer time. I was fooled by your wicked trickery, and left here for dead. Now it is you who must pay the price!"

Taking out his scimitar one more time, my brother struck out at the woman, dashing her into four pieces.

Only the young woman remained in the house. My brother sought her out, and she was greatly affrighted to see him.

"Pray, spare my life, for I am not the instigator of the crimes that you have witnessed here!" the woman pleaded. "I was brought to this place through trickery, as were you. Once, I was the wife of an honest merchant. The old woman came to me, urging me to accompany her to a lavish wedding, which she assured me I would enjoy. Here, I was enslaved by the giant slave, and compelled to do his bidding."

Filled with compassion, my brother agreed to spare the woman's life.

"What riches have been looted from the innocent and are kept here now?" asked my brother.

"There are many thousands of gold coins, and jewels of all kinds," replied the woman. "You may take from these what you will."

My brother then left the house, to gather the support of ten of his friends, who might help him carry this great hoard back to his own residence. However, when he returned, he discovered that the woman had already departed, taking the jewels and the gold with her.

My brother then resolved to take the furniture and tapestries from the house, which he reasoned he could sell for a handsome price. However, his removal of these items involved frequent comings and goings to the house, which alerted the suspicions of the neighbours.

Perceiving him to be a thief, several of the neighbours reported my brother to the magistrate, who sent his guards to arrest him. My brother's attempt to bribe the guards, and his explanation for his actions, fell on deaf ears. And so, my brother was arrested and brought before the magistrate to answer his case.

My brother related his story to the magistrate, describing how he had been originally deceived by the old woman, and that his taking from the house was at the invitation of the younger woman who had resided there.

He begged the magistrate to allow him to keep some of the items that he'd taken, in compensation for the money that had been stolen from him. But the magistrate refused to entertain his request, instead ordering that he must flee the city, and give up his house and all that he owned.

During his exile, my brother was attacked by highwayman, who left him naked by the roadside. I got wind of his misfortune, and ventured to find him. Then I brought him home to my house. Here, I clothed and fed him, and have until now protected him from further harm.

Arcade dreams

I was born into a large family just before the war, the youngest of three girls and four boys. Mum had lost two daughters in childbirth, and within months of me arriving on the scene, was pregnant again. Billy joined our happy family just in time for Christmas.

I don't remember much about those early years in Bow, a few miles east of the City of London. We lived in a modest terraced house close to a railway junction, and I used to share a bed with my two elder sisters.

When the war started, my dad was called up to join the army. He was posted to Canvey Island in the Thames Estuary, where he manned anti-aircraft guns and trained new recruits before they were sent off to face Hitler's armies.

Mum did her best to bring us kids up, but it couldn't have been easy feeding eight mouths when rationing began. Soon there were nine of us, when my grandma moved in with us after her house was dealt a direct strike by a Luftwaffe bomb.

She was lucky to have made it to the shelter at the tube station before the air raid began. Her gas stove didn't fare so well–being carried a full thirty yards by the blast, before being buried under a pile of rubble at the bottom of her garden.

I have only a faint memory of the war. Billy and I were evacuated for a time to live with our aunt in Lincoln, but mum was always worried about the distress that Billy might cause her. The problem was that Billy was different to other kids–a mongoloid, as we used to call people like him, but that was before we knew much about my poor brother's condition.

When he was born, he had a flattened nose and eyes that slanted upwards. He didn't learn to walk until he was three, and was even older before he could pronounce his name. Mum knew from the start that Billy was going to have a tough time making it through life, but she pleaded with the authorities not to take him away from her when they wanted to put him in a special home.

"As long as I've got breath in my body, I'll do my best for Billy," I can remember her saying. Billy used to stare into space for long periods of time, but his cheerful smile always broke our hearts.

When the war ended, the family moved from London to Canvey Island, which dad thought would be a good place for us to build our new lives. We moved into a small house on the edge of the main village on the island, taking grandma with us.

After the rough years of war, coming to Canvey was like arriving in Paradise for us kids. There were acres of grassy fields to play in, lots of strange places for games of hide-and-seek, and–of course–the sea. Actually, what we called the sea was really the Thames Estuary, though it felt like a real sea to us–and had a beach to prove it.

I quickly settled into my new school, making friends with other kids whose families had also decided to break away from London. Dad was working at the docks in Wapping, which involved him catching an early train each morning and arriving home each evening just in time to kiss us younger kids goodnight.

Billy wasn't so lucky. When he reached school age, he started with other kids at the same school as me. But it was soon clear that the school didn't want to care for Billy. He found it hard to make friends, and in an attempt to get attention, soon turned to pulling girls' hair and biting boys' arms. Most of the rest of the time, he refused to pay attention to his teacher, preferring to put on a show of wild screaming, or sitting in the sandpit and covering himself with sand.

The authorities had never been happy when my mum insisted that Billy should go to what she thought was a "normal" school. "It will be much better for Billy," they told her, "If he comes with us to a special place, where he can be given the care that he needs."

Mum was summoned to see the headmistress at least once each week, following another of Billy's tantrums.

"We are running out of last chances for your son, Mrs. O'Brien," the headmistress told her on one visit. "Billy is upsetting other children, and causing too much stress for his teacher. We are going to have to make other arrangements for him."

Mum knew that her battle to give Billy a chance of a proper education was all but over. Her desperate pleas with him to behave and work hard at school had fallen on deaf ears. So it was on one fateful morning in March that two smartly dressed women arrived at our door to take Billy to what they called a hospital in the country. We knew it less politely as the "loony bin".

Mum wept for days after Billy was taken from us. I dearly missed my brother, while I didn't fully understand what was happening at the time. It was only many years later that I learned the truth.

Mum and dad weren't able to get to see Billy very often, since there were no buses that went near the hospital. Normally, they could only visit when my uncle Brian paid us a visit in his shiny Ford Consul.

Even when they were able to visit Billy, one of the hospital nurses was always with them. Billy used to stay silent most of the time mum and dad were with him, but used to cry profusely when they went to leave without him.

Mum used to cry too. I even saw dad shed a tear after some of his visits to the asylum, although he desperately tried his best to console my mum. "I'm sure they know what they're doing, love," he used to say, steadying his embrace around my delirious mum. "Billy's in the best place–that's what we always have to remember."

My parents later told me that, despite always showing a brave face, they felt that they'd betrayed Billy by letting the authorities take him away. We heard all sorts of terrible stories about what went on inside the hospital. Some patients were regularly subjected to electric shocks–a practice that was supposed to help them, but struck me as being a ghastly torture. We heard claims of children being beaten when they had wet their bed, and there were rumours that one girl had even had her face held under the bathwater when she refused to take a wash–not being released from her near-drowning until her face had turned blue.

What was clear was that Billy wasn't allowed to wear his own clothes. He managed to tell us later that the beds in the dormitory were pushed so close to-gether that there was no place for anyone to keep their own clothes near to them. There was one wardrobe at the end of the room, and whoever got their first took whatever clothes they wanted.

Mum and dad were also worried that Billy wasn't eating well. He had lost a lot of weight soon after en-tering the institution, and one of the few words that he ever spoke to them was "bread...please bring bread."

My parents' attempts to speak to someone about Billy's care were given short shrift. When they tried to ask a question, they were usually told that their visit-ing time was over, or that Billy had to go back for his treatment. We tried to carry on with our lives without always worrying about Billy, but he was rarely far from our thoughts.

One incident that did divert our attention for a while occurred one terrifying night in the January of 1953. No one had warned us what was to come, al-though my friends and I had noticed that the water on the far side of the seawall was much higher than at normal high tide. A powerful gale had begun to whip across the island by early evening, and so dad insisted that we all stayed inside the house, where we took to our beds early in an effort to stay warm.

We were woken sometime after midnight by the faint sound of a siren. I could hear dogs barking, and babies crying, although their desperate wailing was barely audible above the roar of the wind. When we looked through the window, we couldn't believe what we saw.

Our street had become a fast-flowing river, carrying with it dining chairs and mattresses, babies' prams and motorbikes with their sidecars still attached. Since our house had two levels, we were able to keep above the level of the water in our bedrooms, which were upstairs. The water flooded everything below, but at least we were safe and had some protection from the freezing wind outside.

Others weren't so lucky. Some of our neighbours had to scramble onto the roofs of their houses, hoping that an army boat would rescue them before the water rose any higher. Mrs. Hughes, one of the older residents in our street, was among those who didn't survive.

She'd managed to crawl onto the roof of her bungalow, although the water's powerful current had almost swept her and the guttering that she was clinging onto into its merciless course. But a worn blanket and flannel nightdress weren't enough to save her from the cold. Like many of the fifty-eight other people whose lives were taken by the storm surge on the island that night, she succumbed to the freezing temperature, rather than being swept under by the violent water.

We lost our dog that night, who'd got shut off in the kitchen, where she normally slept. Penny had been part of our family since we lived in Bow, and I don't think that mum and dad ever forgave themselves for keeping her shut up at night.

After the army rescued us and took us off the island, we were able to appreciate the full scale of the disaster. Large stretches of the Essex coast had been flooded, but nowhere was as badly hit as Canvey.

Following the flood, I was sent to stay with my aunt Eleanor in Lincoln, where I stayed for three months. My aunt had contracted polio at the gas turbine factory where she worked. She found it hard to look after us and had to be careful not to come too close to us when she coughed and sneezed, but we were all able to help with cooking and cleaning.

Dad had to keep working, and so it was my mum who took on the larger part of the task of getting our home back into a state that was fit for us to move into again. We'd lost the few photographs of our early years together in London, while mum's precious vase that had been passed on to her by her grandmother was among the many ornaments in our home that were destroyed.

When mum and dad were able to visit Billy for the first time after the flood, it had been a full six months since they'd last seen him. Mum said that Billy's eyes told her everything she needed to know about his well-being, but she and dad were amazed when he spoke to them more fluently than normal, uttering far more words than he'd ever done before.

"They beat me! They beat me! They beat me!" he cried. "Want to go home! Want to go home! No more! No more!"

"What do they do to you, Billy?" my mum carefully enquired, desperate to disguise her grieving for her son.

"Make me go outside in the nude! Go outside when it's dark!" Billy replied, tears now streaming from his eyes. "Evil here! Evil people!"

The nurse who'd been watching over my parents' conversation with Billy had signalled for other staff to bring help. With their attention fully focused on Billy, my parents didn't notice movements in the background before two men arrived at Billy's side, one of whom was carrying a straitjacket.

"Visiting time is now over, Mr. and Mrs. O'Brien," The nurse curtly instructed my parents. "You will be able to visit your son again in a month's time."

Billy was now screaming, pleading my parents not to leave him alone. "Horrible here! Horrible here!" he shrieked, desperate for his mum and dad to carry him away. But the men who stood behind him took a firm hold on my brother, brutally wrestling him into the suit as he continued to cry out for help.

My parents could barely speak, shocked and disbelieving at what they were witnessing.

"We won't let you down, Son," promised my dad. "We'll get you out of this place very soon, don't you worry!"

"I love you, Billy," my mum cried out as Billy was dragged away from the small table where he'd felt the loving touch of my parents' hands. "I'll never let you down–not as long as I've got breath in my body!"

Were they honest, my parents didn't know what to do. The letter that they wrote to the governor of the asylum, begging him to discharge Billy from institutional care, received a stark and unsympathetic response. Their letter to the hospital board was met with a similar reply.

In desperation, mum and dad arranged a meeting with our MP. Dad brushed down his only suit, and mum put on her Sunday best, hoping to impress this long-standing parliamentarian and convince him that they were worthy to be treated as people who had a high standard of self-respect.

To their surprise, the smart-suited man received them warmly at his constituency office, and appeared to be genuinely interested in their case. "One of my honourable friends, the Minister of Health, is looking at this very issue at the moment," he responded. "My party believes that it's time that we start treating those who are on the margins of our society with a little more dignity, and this is a view that's gaining currency in the House."

Mum and dad were delighted when our parliamentary representative offered to intercede with the governor of the asylum on our behalf, hopeful that he would be more successful than they had been in securing Billy's release.

"Dick and I go back a long way," he revealed, referring to his acquaintance with the governor. "Just you leave this with me, Mr. and Mrs. O'Brien," he said with what my mother feels sure was a wink. "I'll make sure that your son's best interest is made a priority."

We don't know what the MP did, but within three weeks of their meeting with him, my parents received a letter from the asylum informing them that arrangements were being made for Billy's discharge.

We arranged a party in the church hall to celebrate his homecoming. Aunts and uncles from all around came to my dear brother's party, and everyone who lived in our street also joined in the celebration to welcome him home.

Billy slowly revealed the extent of the horrors that he'd endured during his stay in the asylum. He also proclaimed categorically what he wanted to happen to the people who had harmed him.

The punishment that he foresaw involved locking each of the staff members in a padded cell, forcing every one to wear a nightshirt that had been soaked in urine. This had been the punishment suffered by Billy and others when they'd been unable to hold their water. Billy then elaborated on the names that he would scream at his former tormentors as he whipped them. He was sure that they would all profess their sorrow for treating him so badly and agree to become his servants, as he took on the role of the new governor of the asylum.

In Billy's imagination, his former captors would obey his every command, knowing that they would suffer the pain of electric shocks if they did not. The former governor would bow whenever he saw Billy, and not be allowed to speak unless Billy granted him an audience.

The nurses that cursed him would have to sleep outside in the cold, and the wicked people who administered the electric shocks to him would spend their waking hours struggling inside their straitjackets. All the patients who had suffered alongside Billy would be released home to their mums and dads.

We let Billy enjoy the retribution on the hospital that he fantasized about, but knew that he must never set foot in that terrible building again.

One person who was missing from Billy's party was our aunt Eleanor, who was too frail to make the journey from Lincoln. Her polio had caused paralysis in her spine, and she often struggled for breath. Mum visited her once she felt comfortable to leave Billy in the daytime care of his brothers and sisters, staying with her sister for what were to be the last few weeks of aunt Eleanor's life. Mum had not long finished nursing her mum in our own home, just before my grandma passed away.

My aunt's death came as a terrible shock to all of us, even though we knew that her illness had tightened its hold on her during the preceding months. Mum and dad attended her funeral, along with some of my older siblings. They returned with the news that my aunt had left a small sum of money in her will, which was to be shared equally among each of her nieces and nephews.

Mum and dad weren't sure what to do with Billy's share, but they felt that he should be given something to spend for himself. Billy knew little about the value of money, but understood that were he to sensibly invest the Ten Pounds note that dad gave him, he could make even more money, and so have more to invest again, allowing his savings to grow.

Billy was determined to spend all of his money on the coin-pushing machine at the Fantasy amusement arcade along the seafront. We each attempted to discourage him from his plan, but Billy was certain that spending such a large amount of money could only yield him even more.

With the winnings that he earned, Billy intended to buy himself the biggest train set in the world. The locomotives would pant real steam, just like the ones that took dad to work every morning. There would be dozens of sidings, all feeding into a giant turntable wheel. The model cows that would graze in the green-sand fields would all stand alert to watch the ten-carriage expresses passing by.

Billy would be able to control everything from his command position–a large hole carved into the middle of the layout's board. He would wear a signalman's cap and from his perfect vantage point, blow a whistle before turning the knob to set the trains in motion. He would be able to switch any point on the layout to send a train exactly where he wanted it to go.

When he wanted it to be night, street lamps would illuminate, and lights would come on in the houses of the layout's town and two villages. Taxis would wait in their bays outside each station, ready to take travellers home. Ducks would float on the lake in the town's park, where smiling dog walkers would chat with passers-by, as their dogs bounded across the grass to fetch balls and sticks.

The town would have a police station, a church, a pub, and a school. Liveried lorries would deliver their wares to the high street stores, and trolley bus cars would pass each other on the street. A postman would stand by a post box, preparing to empty it of its contents, before racing back to the post office in time for the overnight mail train.

Trains would rush through tunnels and glide over viaducts. A funfair would occupy the green of one of the villages, while a busy market would fill the square of the other.

Billy had worked through every detail of his creation in his mind–even down to what the names of all the streets would be, and the hymn that the choirboys would sing as they made their way from the side-building vestry to the church.

I enjoyed asking Billy to describe the different scenes that would play out in his fantasy world. He was never lost for a colourful and intriguing answer.

Since he would talk of little else, mum and dad eventually agreed to allow Billy to spend a portion of his inheritance on the coin-pushing machine. I went with mum and Billy to watch him make his fortune.

The cash teller almost ran out of penny coins when Billy went to cash his Ten Pounds note. It took all three of us to carry six heavy bags of coppers over to the machine.

One by one, Billy started to send the coins tumbling into the slots of the fascinating apparatus. He was able to choose one of a dozen slots that were evenly spaced across the top of the machine. By this means, he could direct a coin to land on the upper of two moving platforms that slowly nudged the growing quantity of coins that had come to rest on it closer toward its edge.

Occasionally, a coin might land on the upper platform where Billy wanted it. As the platform moved in and out against a plastic wall, a coin brushing against the wall could be enough to dislodge one or more of the coppers that rested in front of it–causing them to tumble onto the lower platform. If the timing was right, these coins could in turn land so as to force other coins to tumble into a collecting tray, where they could be claimed as a prize.

Billy's game with the machine started well. He seemed to have a special sense to know when to drop a coin. Mum and I cheered him on, surprised by his initial success. We applauded him whenever another coin dropped into the winner's tray, but we weren't keeping count of the number of coppers that were being fed into the machine.

Billy was clearly enjoying himself, certain that his growing pile of winning coppers would soon outnumber the pennies that he'd needed to spend to free them from their glass-walled prison. We allowed the winnings to pile up until we took the last coin from the cash bags. Then we counted the winnings. Billy had won just under five pounds.

Disappointed but still trusting that his luck would turn, Billy continued to toss more coins into the machine, while mum and I pleaded with him to not allow himself to lose any more.

When his stock of coins was spent, we again counted his winnings, discovering that his purse had now reduced to only two pounds. Billy remained determined to win over the machine and to earn enough to build his train set, but after several more cycles of collecting his winnings and then feeding them back into the machine, he finally came to his last coin. Billy's dream was over, and he could no longer hold back his dismay.

Billy burst into tears, then started thumping the glass panel that fronted the machine, intent on showing it his anger. Mum attempted to pull Billy away, but he carried on wailing and screaming words that we didn't understand, still thumping and thumping.

In the process of pounding the machine, Billy caused it to part with several stacks of coppers that had been waiting to fall. But his commotion also attracted the attention of the cashier.

Securing the lock on the small cage that served as her office, the concerned woman came running toward us. "What are you doing?" she hollered. "You'll break the glass if you don't stop! Stop right away, or I'll need to call for security!"

The woman's reprimand registered with Billy. He backed away from the machine, clutching my hand and still crying uncontrollably. My mum explained what had happened, and attempted to excuse Billy's behaviour by mentioning his condition. The woman was moved to show a little sympathy, and having seen how much money Billy had wasted on the machine, agreed that he could take a pocket-full of the coins that he'd just displaced, provided we left the arcade immediately.

The debacle had been witnessed by a group of three Teddy Boys, who had been previously engrossed in their attempt to get the better of a *Strike Allwin* penny machine that was alive with flashing lights and fast-spinning ball bearings on the other side of the arcade.

When we made to leave the arcade after our embarrassing dialogue with the cashier, the three drape-jacketed youths followed behind us. Our journey home took us across a small park, where one of the lads suddenly ran from behind, kicking Billy squarely on the backside. This caused the other two pranksters to break into a menacing guffaw, but their companion hadn't finished with his taunting.

"What are you doing out of the loony bin, you half-wit?" he jeered. "Inside is where you're meant to be—not out here, letting your ugly face spoil the scenery."

While she felt close to striking out at the boy, my mother pleaded with him to stop. "Please leave us alone!" she begged. "We don't mean you any harm."

The youth must have heard my mother, but didn't even pass a glance to acknowledge her. He pushed hard on Billy's shoulder. "Crying is all you can do when you lose a gamble, is it, you big baby?" he persisted. "And you need your mum to look after you when you get upset?"

The youth then dealt Billy a strong blow around his cheek. Billy started to run, but the youth quickly caught up with him, and holding out a leg, caused Billy to fall headfirst onto the ground. Mum and I could see that Billy was badly grazed, while a cut was widening up under his right eye.

The gang left us alone at that point, but Billy was determined to have his revenge. When we returned home, he described what he planned to do, as I helped mum dress his wound.

"Teddy Boy not kick me when he see I have knife!" he threatened. "Tomorrow I go to park with knife!"

"No, Billy–No!" screamed my mum. "You must never play with knives. Someone will be badly hurt!" Billy broke out into another fit of sobs, but with mum's and my persuasion, he stopped talking about knives–at least, for the moment.

I promised mum that I would keep an eye on Billy the next day, when she had to go out to buy groceries. I tried to amuse Billy with a game of Ludo but he was lost in one of his spells of distant staring. After I had to leave him alone for a moment to use the bathroom, he was gone.

Billy had returned to the arcade, where he saw the Teddy Boys playing with their machine. "I fight you!" Billy challenged his adversary with as much menace as his voice could manage. "Ten minutes, in park where you hurt me yesterday."

We later learned that the two bystanders in the group attempted to discourage their friend from wasting any more time with Billy. But this pig-headed lout was set on making sure that Billy didn't come to bother him any more.

Billy faced up to his foe. The Teddy Boy baited him to pull the first punch, but when Billy attempted to throw a right hook at the much larger youth, his opponent swiftly grabbed his shirt and pushed him away. Billy struggled to remain standing, and by the time he had steadied himself, the Teddy Boy was moving determinedly toward him, shouting threats and mocking Billy for his condition.

Scared that he was about to face another rough bruising as he hit the ground, Billy reached into his pocket, taking out a knife.

By now, I had found my mum and returned with her to the park, where a small crowd was gathering to watch the unfolding action.

"Billy!" my mother yelled, "Put away the knife! Put it away this instant!"

Billy glanced at my mother, and then faced his opponent once more. The knife that he'd taken from the
cutlery drawer was a butter knife–and fortunately, a
blunt one at that. Still, this was potentially a deadly
weapon when held by the wrong hands. Letting out a
scream that I imagine was meant to be his battle cry,
Billy rushed toward the yob, but letting go of the knife
as he did so.

By a miracle, the knife missed its target, and was
quickly recovered by the youth, who then stood bran-
dishing it in a fresh face-off against Billy. Mum
pleaded with the youth to drop the knife, but he
broadened his smile, and intensified his taunting.

Injury was only prevented when a policeman suddenly pulled up on his bicycle, quickly coming to the
place where the fight was being staged. The officer
had been alerted to the commotion by one of the people in the crowd. Having separated the pair, the
policeman radioed for additional support, and both
Billy and the Teddy Boy were arrested on suspicion of
intent to cause grievous bodily harm.

Both were soon charged with this offence, and told
that they would face trial at Essex Assizes Court. Billy
was released on bail, having spent a traumatic night in
a police cell–which reminded him of his incarceration
in the asylum. We had to wait six months before his
case went to trial.

Mum and dad arranged an appointment to meet our MP once more, although he said that he couldn't concern himself with matters that had yet to go to court. However, he was able to introduce them to a well-respected defence lawyer, whose daughter had a similar disability to Billy's, and who he felt sure would be sympathetic toward his case.

The trial was harrowing for us to observe from the public gallery, but was especially so for Billy, who was called to give evidence in his defence.

Billy's lawyer delivered a masterly performance, educating both the judge and the jury about Billy's condition—what was now beginning to be more properly understood and referred to as Down Syndrome. When their guilty verdict was delivered, the foreman of the jury begged the judge on behalf of his fellow jurors to show leniency toward Billy.

The Teddy Boy was sentenced to twelve weeks in prison, and banned from having any contact with Billy. Billy had his sentence suspended in view of what the judge described as being "exceptional circumstances". He acknowledged the devotion that my parents had shown toward my brother, but warned that he could not prevent him from being sent to prison were he found guilty of similar misconduct in future.

My mother vowed that she would keep Billy within her sight at all times—or, as I remember her saying— "for as long as I have breath in my body".

Afterword

The barber's tales are among the best known of the *Nights*, demonstrating the varying fortunes that result from the different choices each brother takes when investing the money that has come to them.

The fifth brother, Alnaschar, is unaccustomed to having any more than a few dirhams, and so feels as though he has inherited a small fortune. His first action might seem to be a sensible one–to ponder how he might best spend the money, and his plan involves what seems to be an honourable scheme to make good on his investment.

However, Alnaschar's vanity and greed quickly overtake him. It's not enough for him to escape his poverty, to buy a large house, and entertain himself with the company of musicians and dancers, but he needs to prove his new status too.

Perhaps imitating what he perceives as being the privilege of the elite, Alnaschar not only lusts after the vizier's daughter, but intends to keep a high seat in his household, and to rule over every aspect of his wife's life. He wishes to be treated like a prince–to be shown respect by the highest officer of state, as well as by his family and fellow citizens.

This wild fantasising is echoed in the colourful daydreaming of Tevye, the poor milkman whose story

is told in the famous musical *Fiddler on the Roof.* In
the song *If I were a Rich Man*, Tevye dreams of own-
ing a grand house in the centre of the town, filling his
yard with poultry of all kinds, and ordering servants to
satisfy his every whim.

Every detail is worked through in his vision–even
down to his wife having a double chin, and the house
boasting a "spare" staircase that's just for show. He
becomes the one that esteemed men will consult with,
and will spend his days discussing the holy books with
learned rabbis. Of course, Tevye's dream never comes
to fruition, and ultimately an edict of the Tsar forces
him and his family to flee their homeland.

There's nothing wrong in having a dream, nor in
embellishing a vision with rich detail. Those who can
clearly imagine the life that they wish to lead may not
uncommonly end up getting what they wish for.

What sets Alnaschar's vision apart from others is
that it requires others to behave in exactly the way
that he desires. It's one thing to make a request to God
(or to call upon the Universe to provide a desired outcome), but quite another to interfere with the free will
of others.

Alnaschar falls into the trap that deceives many
fantasists–expecting every action, every dialogue, and
every response of others to pan out exactly in the way
that he imagines. He cannot anticipate alternative out-

comes; he inhabits and scripts his fantasy so fully, that it becomes for him all but real.

His disappointment comes quickly when his plan is thwarted even before he has been able to make his first move. Brought back to his senses, Alnaschar berates himself for his vanity and greed, but is soon offered another opportunity to regain what he has lost.

He starts off well, offering hospitality and alms to the old woman who is supposedly on her way to the mosque. But he is soon enticed into a dangerous world, foolishly being led on by the improbable suggestion that a beautiful woman is waiting to marry him.

His money is taken from him, and he is brought to his knees a further time. After taking out his revenge, he shows mercy to the young woman without testing her story. She too soon proves to be unfaithful to her word. His desperate means for regaining the money that he has lost–by stealing furniture and tapestries from the house–leads to further disaster, with his arrest and banishment from the city.

Even when he has nothing left but the clothes he wears, Alnaschar is reduced to nothing by highwaymen. Finally, he becomes dependent on his brother for his protection and survival.

This is a story about a man who never learns that greed leads to inevitable destruction. Whenever he acknowledges this and shows remorse, he is quickly blessed and rewarded.

However, it takes a series of hard lessons–losing his investment and his dream, being left for dead, and finally being stripped naked–to break him down and brought to a point where he might set off on a virtuous path. The story doesn't reveal whether or not he ultimately succeeds in following such a path, but we are left in no doubt about the lesson that we should take from it.

The tale of the young woman and her five lovers

There once lived a young woman, as cunning and knowledgeable in the ways of men as she was beautiful. Her beauty ensnared every man that set eyes on her. She never lacked for suitors, who would answer to virtually any whim in order to win her favour.

Since her husband travelled frequently, this woman could not from time to time resist giving in to the temptations of the flesh. And so it was that at the time our story begins, she was enraptured by a young man's charms.

The young man couldn't always contain his emotion, and following his part in a brawl in the city square, found himself imprisoned at the pleasure of the city's governor. So distressed was the woman at being separated from her lover, that she devised a clever plan to be reunited with him.

Adorning herself in one of her finest robes, she hastened to the governor's mansion, begging that she might be granted an audience with him.

"Oh my Lord," she cried, prostrating herself before the governor's feet, "I beg you to consider the case of my poor brother, who is my only means of support, and who has been unfairly imprisoned by your court."

"He is the victim of a malicious plot," she continued, "And was convicted on the strength of false testimony. I beg you to release him, such that true justice might be served."

The governor took little time to reach his verdict. As soon as he'd cast eyes on the troubled young woman, he had been unable to resist her beauty.

"It will be done," he promised, "But first, my dear woman, attend for me in my harem."

Recognising his motive, the woman cautiously responded, "My Lord, I would gladly do so, however my custom prevents me from entering a stranger's house. If it pleases my Lord, I would be honoured to entertain you at my humble home."

"Where do you reside?" returned the governor.

The woman stated her address, and proposed that he visit her that evening. The governor consented, barely able to conceal his mischievous intention.

The woman then made quickly for the qadi's house, where she repeated the story about her alleged brother's imprisonment at the hands of the governor. She pleaded that the qadi might intervene on her behalf, such that the governor might be urged to overturn the judgement.

"I will be your intercessor," promised the qadi, "But first, please wait for me in my harem."

The qadi's intention was immediately clear to the young woman.

"Sir, I will happily await you there," she offered, "But it would please me more if you would be so gracious as to be entertained in my own home, where there are no slaves nor maidservants who might disturb our privacy."

Unable to believe his good fortune, the qadi promptly agreed to the woman's plan, and it was arranged that he would visit her that evening.

Following this encounter, the woman hastened to the dwelling place of the chief vizier. Again, she pleaded her case for the imprisoned youth, beseeching the vizier's help to secure his release.

"Very well, woman," proclaimed the vizier, "But first bide a little time in my private chamber."

The young woman feigned allegiance, but proposed that she would be most honoured should the vizier prefer to be received in her own house. Eager to make her acquaintance, the vizier promptly agreed to visit her that evening.

At last, the woman proceeded to the palace, where she sought an audience with the king. On entering the great hall of the palace, she fell at the feet of the mighty ruler and implored him, "Your Gracious Majesty, I beg you to consider the case of my brother, who has been wrongly imprisoned on the claims of wicked lies. He is my pillar, my sole provider, and my protector. I beseech you to show mercy, as Your Majesty pleases!"

Seeing the woman, the king was overcome with desire, as had been the reaction of the three distinguished fellows before him.

"I will look favourably on your case," announced the king, "But I desire that you first rest awhile in my private quarters."

"Such a poor servant as myself cannot fail to obey her master," replied the woman, "But, if Your Majesty allows, it would render me the greatest honour were your greatness to visit my humble home, for I do not feel worthy to enter your royal rooms."

On hearing this, the king let out a roar of laughter. But being gratified by the thought of seeing the young woman alone, he consented to visit her that evening.

Finally, the woman stopped by a carpenter's shop, where she left instructions for a fine piece of furniture to be made for her, which was to be delivered to her home before evening that day. "I need a tall cupboard, containing four large containers stacked on top of each other, and capable of being secured with sturdy locks."

When she asked the carpenter what price she must pay for his work, she was told, "Such a piece will cost ten dirham, but if you are happy to step into the back room of my shop, I will gladly waive my fee."

Seeing that she had also seduced the carpenter, the woman proposed that he should visit her later that evening. She then revised the detail of her commission, saying that the cupboard should include five equally sized compartments rather than four.

The woman then hurried home, where she collected four very strangely shaped and poorly sewn garments, which she proceeded to take to a dyer's shop. Here, she arranged for each garment to be dyed in the most outrageous colours, then returned to her house in order to prepare for the evening.

She draped fine satins over her couch, and lit scented candles. The smell of sweet incense filled her room, while perfumed flowers added their precious aroma to the warm and comforting air. Just before evening, the woman arranged her hair, and put on a brightly coloured nightdress.

Just in time for her evening's appointments, a porter delivered the completed cupboard to her room.

The first visitor to arrive was the qadi. After leading him into her chamber, she bowed low before him and showered him with compliments.

"My master, how it delights me for you to come to my simple home," she began, "What a wonderful experience awaits us this evening!

"My Lord, forgive me to suggest that it will comfort you more if you slip off your clothes and take on this simple nightshirt that belongs to my husband," she continued.

The qadi, lost in his love for his hostess, unhesitatingly obeyed, putting on the peculiar habit in place of his smart attire.

After accepting wine and grazing on luscious fruits, the qadi placed his broad arm around the shoulders of the woman, starting to draw her closer toward him. As he played with her hair and breathed kisses on her cheek, a loud knock on the door announced the arrival of a visitor.

"Who might this be at this late hour?" the qadi enquired.

"It must be my husband, returning sooner than I'd expected!" the woman replied. "Quick, you must hide!"

Hurriedly, the woman ushered the qadi toward the cupboard, imploring him to squeeze into the lowest of its five compartments. Once he had crawled inside, she shut the compartment door and fastened its lock. She then raced to the door to welcome her next guest.

The governor now stood before her, who received her bows and plaudits, before he was led into her chamber.

"Let me pour you a drink and offer you a little nourishment," she urged. "I beg that you free yourself from your heavy clothes, and try on this simple vestment belonging to my husband, which is more fitting for a night of merrymaking."

The governor followed her suggestion, swapping his clothes for the ridiculous garment that the woman handed to him.

"Before we venture further," the woman motioned, "Might I ask Your Excellency for the warrant for my brother's release, which you promised?"

Duly, the governor added his seal to the document that would secure the youth's release.

Seated on the couch, the pair began to frolic with each other. The governor's embrace tightened, his whispers became more amorous, and his kisses were offered ever more passionately as he felt himself approaching a moment of ecstasy.

Soon, there again came a knocking on the door.

"This must be my husband arriving home far sooner than he'd informed me!" cried the woman. "Quick! He cannot see you here, lest he beat me and throw me out onto the street!"

The woman ushered the governor toward the cupboard, urging him to conceal himself in the compartment above that which housed the qadi. Once he was inside, she closed the door and secured its lock.

The third visitor–the vizier–was welcomed in the same manner as the two previous guests. As had they, he was easily persuaded to remove his fine vestments in favour of the ridiculous, cheap garment that the woman presented to him.

As the pair prepared to enjoy each other's company, they were interrupted by a loud knock on the door. The vizier was led to the middle compartment of the cupboard, soon finding himself locked in a small space–just like the other two rascals who were trapped below him.

The woman greeted the king's arrival with a full display of deference.

"Your Majesty, I am beyond words to describe my honour in receiving your visit to my humble home," she began. "May your humble servant not displease you with my modest entertainment."

"If it pleases Your Majesty, might I suggest that you take off your royal garb, and receive this simple gift from my husband's wardrobe?"

While he might normally fly into a rage at the mention of such a presumptuous proposal, the king's longing to satisfy his passion impelled him to adopt the common man's dress, even though it was worth no more than a few dirhams.

Suddenly, a loud knocking announced the arrival of another visitor.

Appearing suddenly agitated and afraid, the woman cried out, "Oh my life, my husband is returning! He must not find us together! Please, Your Majesty, allow me to protect your privacy. Please step inside this cupboard, where you will not be found."

The king hurried into the fourth compartment, hearing the lock clicking shut as the door closed behind him.

The woman proceeded to open the house door to greet the carpenter, the fifth of her expected guests.

No sooner had she led the carpenter into the house, than she exclaimed, "Oh hopeless carpenter, what an unsuitable work you have fashioned for me! Your cupboard is formed with an upper container that can hold next to nothing, not being of equal size to the others as I ordered!"

"I cannot agree," responded the carpenter, "Assuredly, the container is large enough to hold both myself, and two others of my size besides!"

"Then prove this to me!" demanded the woman, leading the carpenter to the cupboard that he'd crafted earlier that day.

The carpenter mounted the cupboard, then stepped into the upper compartment. No sooner had he entered into the cupboard than the woman closed the door on him, sealing the lock.

With the five men now captured, the woman made haste to the city's prison. There, she requested an audience with the superintendent, to whom she presented the warrant for the youth's release. Reunited with her lover, she quickly related the strange series of events that had unfolded earlier that day, and warned that they must both make haste to leave the city.

The pair returned to her house, gathered their valuables, and then took flight for a foreign kingdom.

Back in the woman's house, the five captives kept their cover for three full days and three full nights. Without food or drink, and still holding their water, they each waited silently, unaware of the others' presence, and expecting their imminent release.

In time, the carpenter could no longer hold back his toilet. His urine seeped through the floor of his box into the compartment below him, in which the king was crouching. The king in turn opened his bladder, adding to the trickle of water that seeped through into the middle container. The vizier and governor in turn started to leak, causing a torrent to fall down on the poor qadi, who was crouching in the lowest of the five containers.

"Perish this act!" screamed the qadi. "I have suffered enough in this place, without needing to be doused with foul water from above!"

Realising that they were not alone in their hiding places, the governor and vizier then let their voices be heard.

"This most wretched of women has tricked us all! May she perish for her iniquity!" cried the vizier.

Recognising the other's voices, the governor continued, "We–great officers of state–have fallen victim to her evil ways. But thanks be to Allah that our glorious king has been saved this great indignity!"

The king then made himself known, lamenting, "I wish that were so, but I too was led astray!"

The men debated how they might escape their predicament, but could devise no plan for freeing themselves.

After some time, observing that no one had entered or left the house for several days, neighbours became suspicious that something was awry. Taking account of the situation, they resolved that they must investigate the strange circumstance, lest they be accused by the city's authorities of being negligent.

"Let us break entry," proposed one of the neighbours. And so a small group of men set about forcing open the door of the woman's house. Coming inside, the neighbours quickly noticed the large cupboard, from which the muffled wailings of men could be heard.

"It is possessed of jinn!" exclaimed one of the neighbours. "These powerful bodies have been known to take on the form of men, and are able to accurately impersonate their voices!'"

The small gathered group proposed that they must burn the cupboard, but their suggestion was met with a loud plea from the qadi. "Do not burn us alive!" he pleaded, "We are not jinn as you perceive, but men who have been entrapped by a devious woman."

The qadi cried out some verses from *The Qur'an*, which gave the neighbours heart to draw closer to the cupboard. The qadi then explained all that had happened.

After hearing the men's story, the neighbours quickly called for another carpenter, who was able to force open the cupboard's locks, freeing the five from their imprisonment.

Standing together in the room, the men who had been so completely fooled could not help falling into hysterical laughter when they saw each other's dress. They each then put back on their own clothes, and returned to their homes.

High flyers

Gerry was not the most attractive of men, but he possessed an aura that commanded attention. I felt inadequate in his presence, conscious that his sharp wit and strong intellect far outshone mine, but also somehow feeling ungrounded whenever I came near him.

Our considerable age difference might have played a part in the awe that I felt for the man. More probably, our widely separated professional ranks contributed most to my lack of confidence in his presence. He was a managing partner in the large accountancy firm where I worked; I was a mere junior accountant.

Gerry's path to power had been rapid. Yorkshire-born, he excelled at charming and engaging clients. From early in his career, he had consistently beaten the sales targets that were set for him, bringing the firm much needed new business and ever larger and more prosperous assignments. Even before his thirtieth birthday, he had been made a partner.

It was clear that Gerry wasn't satisfied with just being the head of one of the largest divisions in the company's multinational empire. His immediate ambition was to convince his fellow directors that the organisation would be better served if it created a new position of Chief Operating Officer, for which he proposed himself as being ideally suited for the role. And then—well, maybe it would just be a matter of time before the top job became available.

I have no contact with Gerry now. Indeed, both of us have left the company where we met. I took up a position as an accountant for a rival firm. I've no idea what furrow he is ploughing now—and if I'm honest, I don't really care.

My first contact with Gerry was when he engaged me to work on a new assignment that he'd sold to one of his long-standing clients. I didn't report directly to him, and rarely saw him, but whenever he visited the account team, he would take time to speak with each of us individually.

While I felt nervous in his presence, he seemed keen to put me at ease, speaking calmly and with great charm. He would ask for my opinions on different matters relating to the progress of the project and compliment my work–though I doubt he'd really spent any time to note what I'd produced.

At times, even in the very briefest of conversations that we had, he appeared to take me into his confidence, complaining about his fellow directors, and offering his views on some of my colleagues. I was flattered to be appreciated by him, but later learned that this was a style that he adopted with everybody.

I bonded well with my project colleagues, and worked conscientiously to deliver what was expected of me. I must have made a good impression, because I was awarded the top score when I was given my yearly appraisal. This was a rare accolade–something reserved for the few who were regarded as being especially gifted.

Gerry seemed particularly keen to congratulate me for my achievement, and proposed to take me for a celebratory dinner at some posh restaurant in Knightsbridge–a place that was supposedly one of London's most exclusive eateries.

I didn't interpret the smiling glint in Gerry's eye as anything other than a cordial appreciation for my efforts. I had been charmed by this alluring glance before. To be offered the time of one of the most powerful men in the company, ostensibly as a formal acknowledgement and mark of thanks for my work, was something that I didn't feel able to refuse.

Gerry had a stocky composition, and I assumed that he enjoyed eating well. So it proved when we met for our date. He picked his way through no less than five courses, and offered me his recommendations, as he could see that I was someone who was unaccustomed to dining at a Michelin star restaurant.

The wine flowed freely–at least into Gerry's wine glass. Naturally, the waiter sought his opinion rather than mine to confirm that the wine was suitable before pouring. More than a few expensive bottles were brought up from the cellar to keep Gerry satisfied.

"Let me recommend the Merlot, Juliette," offered Gerry, keen to show off his expertise in the art of wine appreciation. "A velvety red, with a plummy aroma, intensely luscious to the taste, with a lingering finish. I always have a glass or two whenever I come here!"

I accepted only small samples from his recommendations, being considerably more restrained in my consumption than was he. I cannot begin to imagine how much the bill that he was running up came to, but that would be taken care of by his seemingly limitless expense account.

We chatted for a long time about all manner of things–not just the business of the office, but about wine, politics, and Abstract Expressionism art, for which Gerry displayed a keen interest.

Between his many anecdotes and attempts at light humour, Gerry quizzed me about my personal life. He seemed particularly interested to learn about my background, my relationships, and my hopes for the future. I told him most of what he wanted to know, but did my best to sidestep his inquiring into my relationships. "You work me too hard to allow much time for things like that!" I teased him, and he seemed content not to press me any more.

By the end of our meal, conversation had returned to focus on my work, and my future in the company.

"I am trying to see how we might better use your talents," Gerry disclosed to me. "How do you feel about taking on the lead of a new job that we're about to kick off?"

I was flattered to be presented with the idea of taking on a role that would involve me having new responsibilities.

"The role would involve a step up the ladder," Gerry explained, "But I'm sure I could put in a good word for you when the promotions are next being discussed."

I could hardly believe what was I was hearing. Not only had I been treated to an exclusive meal, been showered with compliments and charmed by a witty and powerful man, but also a position that I craved now seemed to be but a hair's breadth from my grasp.

Not being able to hide my excitement, Gerry suggested that I might like to continue our discussion at his penthouse in Chelsea Harbour, which was just a short cab ride away. Buoyed by the moment, and not considering that there was anything untoward about his suggestion, I enthusiastically agreed.

Within a short time, I was sitting on a black leather couch in Gerry's apartment, staring out over the Thames, and the myriad blurry lights of the city beyond. The side of the apartment that faced the river was made fully from glass, but with its perfect insulation, not a sound was let through from outside.

The room was quite bare, apart from a few impressive artworks that were hung along the sidewalls, obviously of high quality—and of the Abstract Expressionism genre, I would conjecture. A marble statue of a leopard graced the polished black-slate tiles of the floor on one side of the couch. On the other stood another intricately sculpted bust, which I assumed to be of Heracles, or some other great character from the time of the Classics.

Gerry had busied himself in the kitchen, having discarded his suit jacket and tie. He returned with a pair of champagne glasses, and a magnum of Louis Roederer Cristal.

"I knew there was something that I'd forgotten!" he joked. "What kind of celebration would this be without us cracking open a bottle of bubbly?"

He prized out the bottle's cork with the dexterity of an expert, causing the fizzing liquid to overflow with its customary flare. We raised our glasses, and I accepted his toast–to my future success.

I began to ask Gerry to tell me more about the new project that he had in mind for me, but he now seemed less enthusiastic to discuss the matter than he had been at the restaurant earlier.

"That can wait, my dear, for tomorrow or some other time," he murmured dismissively. "There'll be plenty of time to talk about that. Right now is the time for me to show appreciation for all the good work that you've done!"

No one at the office had called me "my dear" before. This wasn't the language of a professional. I began to wonder how I might tactfully take my leave, not wishing to appear ungrateful for Gerry's hospitality, nor to cause him to have second thoughts about the new role that he had in mind for me. Still, it was clear that Gerry was tired, and quite probably was beginning to feel the effects of all the wine that he'd been drinking.

Gerry had sat down on the large couch, initially respecting a space between us. He turned his attention to the quality of the champagne, then began to point out distant landmarks on the skyline ahead of us, seemingly forgetting that as a Londoner, I was very capable of distinguishing between the Palace of Westminster and the London Eye.

Gradually, Gerry edged nearer toward me. Then, without warning, he placed one of his broad arms around my shoulders, his hand coming to rest in a squeeze on my arm, while his other hand still clutched his glass.

Quickly finishing his drink, he threw the glass across the room, where it quickly shattered into a jig-saw of blade-sharp pieces. "The cleaner can deal with that in the morning!" he chuckled to himself, although I didn't share his amusement.

The force with which he threw the glass made clear his physical strength, and I knew that were he to tighten his grip on me, I would be powerless to resist him.

Relieved of his glass, Gerry let his free arm hover over the front of my body, his hand coming to rest on my right breast. Now increasing the push of his bulky frame against me, I felt his grip tightening, and my nostrils became irritated by the smell of his alcohol-rich breath.

"Come closer, young lady," he whispered. He then landed a disgusting kiss on my right cheek.

With a strength that seemed to come from no-where, I pushed his sweating face away, managing to free myself from his clutches. Without saying a word, I gathered my bag and ran out of the apartment.

Shaking, but still in control of my senses, I quickly found a cab, then ran up the stairs to my apartment, double locking the door and dragging a heavy side table behind it. I vainly hoped that this might give me some protection from any drunken perverts that might be wandering nearby. I slipped off my shoes, threw myself onto my bed, and burst into tears.

I didn't go into the office the next day, nor for any of the five days that followed. Having confided what had happened with my best friend Annie–who had joined the same firm at the same time as me–I resolved to put my dignity ahead of my career prospects, determining to call Gerry to account for what he had done.

When I returned to the office, Gerry seemed unchanged by the events that had played out in his apartment. He made a point of ignoring me, although occasionally addressed me in a professional but not unfriendly manner. As far as I could tell, it seemed to Gerry as though our private evening together had never happened. Not fully to my surprise, Gerry's promise to continue our discussion about the new role that he'd suggested was never followed through.

I realised that Gerry held a very powerful position in the firm, and would be well able to make life difficult for me should he wish to. He was well regarded by the other powerbrokers of the organisation–who shared spacious offices alongside his on the seventh floor, indulged a similar penchant for luscious wine, and accompanied him to watch football from the firm's box at Chelsea.

The pride that I'd felt after my appraisal, and the boost that Gerry's compliments gave me at the restaurant, was short lasting. My experience in Gerry's apartment had left me feeling cold, insecure about my job, and uncertain about what course of action I should take.

I felt helpless to stand up against the might of a popular and apparently invincible business champion such as Gerry. Yet, treading carefully and thoughtfully, I began to devise a scheme that might put the beast in his place.

I resisted the temptation to rush to tell my tale to HR. I felt certain that the HR director–who I knew to be one of Gerry's cronies–would swiftly put a cap on my complaint, and then I would feel all the more aggrieved and unsure which direction I could take. Instead, I began to talk through a plan with Annie.

Annie and I were more than friends. While we had kept this a secret from our colleagues, we had recently begun a relationship together, and had plans to set up home together when the opportunity allowed. I'd never had particular strong feelings for guys, which made Gerry's approach all the more unsavoury for me.

Annie was more outgoing than me. She spent far less time in the office, preferring to occupy her leisure hours in cocktail bars and at parties. She also enjoyed taking part in an amateur dramatics group. In my opinion at least, she could have made a successful ca-

reer as an actress had she not become an accountant.
On top of everything, she was beautiful and had a viva-
cious personality.

Like me, Annie was assigned to one of Gerry's account teams. As he did when he visited our team,
Gerry offered Annie and her colleagues the opportunity for a private audience with him whenever he
passed by. Knowing that he was due to pay her team a
visit, Annie sent him an email, requesting a meeting
with him to discuss a private matter.

Gerry readily agreed to her request, setting aside
extra time to speak with her. Applying her best effort
to appear troubled, Annie related a story to Gerry,
pretending to have been recently ditched by her former boyfriend. She embellished the story with all
manner of details, claiming that she had set her heart
on marrying this man, and that the stress of their parting was proving almost too difficult to contain.

"I'm so sorry to bring this to you," she confessed to
Gerry, "But I fear that if I don't talk about it, my work
will begin to suffer, and you are someone that I feel I
can trust."

Gerry was easily taken in by her story. According
to Annie, he even appeared to be affected by her distress. As we'd hoped, Gerry said that he was more than
willing to act as a sounding board for her, and suggested that they plan a time for a further meeting. As
we'd assumed, the idea of offering his strong, paternal

counsel to a beautiful young woman in distress appealed to his sense of status.

"That is something that will be very helpful to me," Annie lied, "But I wonder if it's something that you might consider offering off-site, because I'm very conscious of the attention others will give me if they see me taking up too much of your time?"

Gerry was happy to suggest meeting at a neutral venue such as a coffee shop, but Annie pushed back, saying that she would feel most comfortable were Gerry ready to meet her in her own home. While this was an unusual request, Gerry consented, and a time was arranged for his visit.

With the first part of our plan complete, Annie and I waited eagerly for Gerry's visit. The next stage of our little scheme involved me hiding in a cupboard out of sight of Gerry, while Annie attempted to persuade him to sit beside her on a couch that faced the cupboard. Here, she would engage him in conversation, continuing her forlorn pretence.

Before the evening of his expected visit, we set up a tiny web camera, which was focused on the couch. Being partially hidden by a tall vase, the camera was barely noticeable. We had concealed the cable linking the camera to my laptop computer, which I planned to use to record Gerry's antics while I hid in the cupboard.

Following his day in the office, Gerry arrived at Annie's flat at the agreed time. When we heard the doorbell ring, I took up my position in the cupboard, settling down with my laptop to set the recording in motion. The camera had a particularly sensitive microphone, and so was able to clearly pick up on all of Gerry and Annie's conversation. I was able to monitor the dialogue using a pair of headphones, while watching their movements in a small window on my computer.

Annie adopted her mournful look, opened the door to Gerry, and led him to the couch.

"You have a great little place here!" Gerry offered, although he was unlikely to be accustomed to being entertained in such humble surroundings. "I could make do with a little more space," Annie replied, "But that will have to wait for a little while."

"Maybe that won't need to be very long," Gerry responded. "From what I hear, your work is going well. I'm sure I can put in a good word for you when it comes to promotion time."

Keen to not allow her glum appearance to slip, Annie proposed making Gerry a drink. This allowed her to escape to the kitchen, where she broke into a broad smile. She later told me that she had had to restrain herself from falling into hysterics, but this clever actress managed to keep her calm.

In Annie's company, Gerry had to content himself with coffee rather than premium wine or champagne. When she returned, he proceeded to ask her about how she was dealing with her breakup, promising to offer any support that he could.

Annie embroidered a fantastic story about how she had been unable to sleep since her supposed boyfriend had abandoned her, making out that her heartache was made worse by the suggestion that she had been jilted in favour of one of her best friends.

She put on a convincing act, even managing to shed a few tears at one point. But Annie's next move nearly caused me to break into helpless laughter, which would surely have given my cover away.

Clutching her still undrunk mug of coffee, Annie feigned nervous panic, as though she were shaking uncontrollably. In the process, she managed to spill most of the contents of her mug over Gerry's custom-tailored suit.

"I'm so sorry! I'm so sorry!" Annie exclaimed. "Let me at once find you a towel to dry yourself with, and a dressing gown to wear, while I rinse and dry your clothes!"

Gerry seemed unsure how to react, but his clothes were drenched through, and so reluctantly he took off his jacket, shirt and pants, handing them to Annie to put in soak. He declined her offer to put on a pink towelling robe, preferring instead to sit virtually naked next to my mischievous chum.

Annie continued to pour out her woes, saying that it would please her were Gerry willing to give her a reassuring hug, "Just like my dad used to do when he was around."

Gerry threw his arm around Annie, as he had done to me, pulling her closely to his side. "Everything is going to be all right," he whispered to her. "Someone as beautiful as you will always go far. Keep coming to me, and I'll make sure that you're looked after!"

Gerry tightened his embrace on Annie, reaching across to kiss her on the cheek. Annie had expected this, and was ready to suffer a little of Gerry's dallying for the good of our plan. He dropped his arm from clutching her shoulder to rest at the top of her thigh, then turned again to plant a couple more pecks on her cheek. Not seeing her resist, he then moved closer to land a kiss directly on Annie's mouth.

I let the camera record his hand slowly creeping up from Anne's thigh to feel the soft surface of her stomach. I concluded at that point that my friend had endured enough. Bringing the recording to an end, I burst out of my hiding place, crying out with as much menace as I could muster, "Get your hands off her, you pervert! You're not going to abuse her the way that you abused me!"

Gerry was stunned by my appearance, and was for once lost for words.

"You see that innocent looking thing up there?" I continued, pointing to the camera. "That's hooked up to a computer. Everything that's gone on here has been recorded! We've got a bit of editing to do, but rest assured, this is going to go viral on YouTube!"

Gerry sat motionless, unable to comprehend what was happening. Annie slipped off to the kitchen, ostensibly to dry out Gerry's clothes, but in reality to set in motion another computer recording, which picked up on a wireless microphone that was hidden behind the couch.

"Of course, HR don't have to hear about this," I continued. "But I want to hear you say "sorry", and never try to abuse your position to get the better of me or my friend again!"

Gerry promised that he would make sure that Annie and I were well treated, and that we could rely on his support at the office.

Before letting him go, I pressed Gerry to name all of our colleagues whom he'd entertained in his apartment. He listed no fewer than six others who'd preceded me. Checking her computer to make sure that this information was being recorded, Annie then stopped the recording, returning from the kitchen with both Gerry's clothes and her computer in hand.

Hurling the still wet clothes at Gerry, Annie teased, "Pity you didn't try on that dressing down–that would have been quite a picture to post on Facebook if we'd had to! Still, I think we've got enough to make sure that you don't forget your promise!" She then pressed the play button on her computer screen, setting in motion a playback of the new recording that she'd made.

In the weeks following his adventure, Gerry treated Annie and myself with kid gloves. I was recommended for promotion soon after, but decided to part company with the firm.

Gerry resigned his post some months later. I don't know what reasons he gave for his parting, but I like to think that Annie and I played a part in his decision. My relationship with Annie has gone from strength to strength. We haven't yet had to return to listen to those recordings of Gerry, but perhaps one time after a bottle of bubbly, we'll sit back and enjoy listening to Annie's star-turn once more.

Afterword

What are we to make of a story in which a young woman sets out to trick some of the most powerful men in the land, in an effort to secure the release of a lover whom she was bewitched by while her husband was away?

In keeping with the view that Scheherazade–the great weaver of the stories of the *Nights*–is the most clever and erudite of women, the subject of this story might be regarded as a similar example of her kind. Others claim that the tale is primarily a satire on the corrupt nature of bureaucrats[11].

Perhaps the storyteller's intention is to prove that women are at least equal to men in their guile and ability to achieve their will, expose hypocrisy, and educate their audience? In the case of Scheherazade, her aim may be to show the tyrant Shahryah that women are not as foolish nor inadequate as he might assume.

This is by no means a universally held point of view. Many feminists might argue that the woman in the story is a harlot–a poor example of womankind, who flaunts her body in order to gratify her carnal needs. Taking another perspective, a woman's power to seduce can be seen as a gift rather than a vice.

It's not clear whether the woman's quest to bring about the release of her lover is justified. We don't know whether the young man was an aggressor in the brawl, nor whether the trial that convicted him was flawed. This isn't the point: the woman is set on eloping with the youth, and is ready to risk any price to

---

[11] See, for example, Dawood, N. J. (translator) (1954) *Tales from the Thousand and One Nights*, Penguin, p 12.

achieve this. Whether it is blind and reckless, or a power that kindles the greatest inventions, love is her main driver.

She sets off with a clear plan, which she executes with precision. Taking every opportunity to demonstrate her influence over the men that she encounters–managing to avoid paying for the carpenter's work–she exudes supreme confidence and cunning. The ultimate price that she would pay were she to fail must have been obvious to her.

It might have been enough for her to have entrapped the governor. Once his authority to release the youth had been obtained, she need not petition any others. However, she deliberately courts the affections of not only the governor, but three other powerful men of state, including the king himself.

Perhaps her intention is to exert revenge on the hierarchy that dominates her society, if not to point out the real weakness of these powerful men. In response to the state having taken away the freedom of her beloved, she resolves to take away the freedom of the state's main powerbrokers.

These are all men–all gullible, all ready to cast off their rich robes in order to satisfy their passions, falsely believing that they remain in control. They totally give in to their carnal natures; their high status can't save them from falling foul in their actions. As the great novelist William Makepeace Thackeray famously put it, "love makes fools of us all"[12].

For a moment, when the neighbours suspect that the cupboard contains jinn, their very lives are at stake. For three days and three nights, they crouch in their compartments, virtually naked, without food or drink, and even afraid to pass water. It is only by a reciting of words from *The Qur'an*–by returning to the morality of their faith–that they are saved.

The carpenter, a common man, is drawn into the same mess that the other four men find themselves in, but he is allowed to retain his clothes (or the face that he normally presents to the world). The others are dressed as figures of fun, fools to be mocked and laughed at. Ultimately, this is what they each realise, embarrassed by their situation, but aware that they have each been as foolish as the other.

For a brief moment, the assembly of men at the end of the story presents all of the men as equals. They see each other's true selves, exposed and naked. How this might change the relationship dynamic among them moving forward is left for only our imagination to conceive. However, we are told that they put their own

---

[12] William Makepeace Thackeray, in *Delphi Complete Works of William Makepeace Thackeray (Illustrated)*, 2013, Delphi Classics.

clothes back on, and so might assume that they will soon return to their old ways.

Exposure is threatening, but when the absurdity of the pretensions that we play out in life are put under the spotlight, we can do little but to smile at our fragility. Revealing ourselves, or–as in this tale–being revealed, can be liberating. Sometimes, it takes an uncomfortable experience to come to a point where we can open up about and come to recognise our true selves.

Aladdin and the wonderful lamp

Once in a city in China there lived a young boy named 'Alā' ad-Dīn, who we may also know as Aladdin. He was a very lazy boy–refusing to take notice of his father or mother when they asked for his help, and spending most of his time playing in the streets with other idle boys like himself, flittering away time with trivial games.

When he reached the age of fifteen, Aladdin's father begged him to set his mind on more profitable activities, offering to educate him in the skills of a tailor, which was his own profession. Stubbornly, Aladdin showed no interest in his father's suggestion, nor in accepting his support to find another way of acquainting himself with some other occupation. At length, the poor old man died, leaving Aladdin's mother to provide for her only son.

"Oh you useless child!" cried his mother. "We are among the poorest in the city, and I must now spin cotton as our only means for making a living. You never help your poor mother, nor show any interest in contributing to the family purse!"

Aladdin was unaffected by his mother's scolding, and continued to while away his hours, joining in with the mischief and street games of his friends.

One day, there came a man from North Africa, who, upon seeing Aladdin, felt certain that he had found just the boy he was looking for. The man—a Moor who was well acquainted with the practices of divination and magic—had travelled across continents to seek out this very child.

After questioning some of the boys who were in the neighbourhood to discover Aladdin's name and his family circumstance, the man then approached the boy, bowing down at his feet.

"At last I have found you, my dear friend!" announced the man, feigning tears and putting on a show of great emotion. "Aladdin, my dear brother's son, how far I have travelled to find you!"

Aladdin was astonished by this display, since he hadn't before been told that his father had a brother.

"I know of no uncle," Aladdin replied. "Tell me, what is your business?"

The man proceeded to explain that he had been abroad for many years, and that perhaps this was the reason why his father had never mentioned their connection before. He said that he had felt that he must journey to see his brother once more, and to make acquaintance with his fine family.

Handing Aladdin a silver coin, the stranger beseeched the boy to tell his mother that her husband's brother had returned, and that if she would so honour him, he wished to be received by her the following evening.

Aladdin relayed the magician's request, but suspecting trickery, his mother was dumbfounded to know who this strange man might be. "Your father did have a brother," she told her son, "But he passed from this life many years ago." Nevertheless, she agreed to entertain the alleged relative, and made ready a supper for his visit the following evening.

The Moor arrived at the poor woman's house at the agreed time, bringing with him several baskets that were filled with fruit and fine meats. He shed tears when accepting the welcome of his cautious hostess, claiming that it had long been his perfect dream to be reunited with his family.

Following an evening of charming conversation, the man promised to treat Aladdin as though he was his own son, affording him whatever help he needed in order to secure a profitable future. Learning that Aladdin yet had no trade, he offered to stock a shop for him, where the boy might try his hand as a merchant. Promising to set about his enterprise the very next day, the man bid his hosts goodnight, insisting that they take a further silver coin from him as a gift.

The following day, the man returned early to escort Aladdin around the city, to search for a suitable premises where the boy might establish his new venture. The Moor showed his newly adopted nephew sights that he'd never seen before, spoke kindly to him, and bought him a fine suit of clothes—one that Aladdin deemed appropriate for his new status as a merchant of the city.

Returning home, Aladdin found that his mother was impressed by his day's adventure, and she began to accept that the strange newcomer might in truth be her husband's brother.

So it was that Aladdin's mother gave her blessing for her son to venture out of the city the following day, such that his new-found uncle might show him some of the great wonders that lay beyond there.

The man led Aladdin far from the city walls, farther than the boy had ever travelled before. They visited fine gardens, and feasted on wholesome food, but Aladdin soon became weary from his many hours of walking, and he begged his uncle that they might turn for home.

Still, the magician's conversation engaged the boy, and he was spurred on to continue along the path by the man's promise that they would soon have sight their destination.

Finally, they came upon a narrow valley, which dissected two steep mountains. "We have come at last to the point where we may rest," said the Moor. "Gather some sticks so that we may light a fire, and then I will show you something that will be unlike anything you've witnessed before!"

Once the fire had been lit, the magician threw some powder that he had brought with him into it, whilst muttering some strange, magical words.

Once he had uttered his spell, the whole earth started shaking, causing some of the sod in front of the two figures to disperse. This cleared way to reveal a flattened stone. The stone was marked at its centre by a brass ring, which allowed it to be lifted–as though it were a lid that might be used to seal a large vessel.

Aladdin was terrified at what he saw, and made as to flee. But the Moor restrained him and dealt him a blow to the face that laid him flat out on the ground.

Using magic to revive him, the magician spoke to reassure the boy, "Fear not, grandson of my father! Once you were a boy, but now you are a man!"

The Moor proceeded to caution Aladdin to obey him, telling him that he must lift the stone, beneath which he would discover a hidden treasure.

"Do as I say," continued the magician, "And half of what you find will be yours!" Then, speaking more forebodingly, he continued, "If you fail, you will at once be finished!"

Excited by the prospect of recovering real treasure, Aladdin took note of everything the magician told him. He was to proceed through an open door at the foot of the steps that led from below the stone, where he would discover three large rooms. "Do not touch anything there, even with your gown," warned the magician, "Or you will surely meet your end!"

The man told Aladdin that the rooms led into a garden, which was graced with a beautiful orchard. He was to continue walking until he sighted a niche in a terrace, where he would find a lighted lamp. The magician instructed the boy to empty the lamp of its oil, and then to quickly bring it back with him.

Aladdin complained that he would not be able to lift the stone alone, but the man assured him that he would accomplish this with ease. To protect him, the magician placed a ring in Aladdin's hand, then bade him to make haste with his mission and prosper.

Aladdin lifted the stone without trouble, and made his way through the three rooms into the garden.

Everything he saw was exactly as the magician had described it.

Approaching the niche where the lamp stood, Aladdin collected some fruit from the trees of the orchard, filling his pockets with his pickings. He then hurried with the lamp back to the entranceway to the large underground chamber, whereupon the Moor immediately demanded that he hand over the lamp.

Now it happened that the magician had let slip the motive for his journey to China. Through divination, he had discovered that a great treasure could be found at the place where the two now found themselves, but that the entrance to its secrets could only be opened—and it's finest treasure retrieved—by a boy named Aladdin, coming from the very city from which they'd come.

The lamp, the Moor had revealed, held the power to make its holder the richest person in the world.

Aladdin now realised that it was not an uncle that had brought him to this mysterious place, and he feared that the man would abandon him as soon as he handed the lamp to him. So he resolved not to hand over the lamp until he was standing on firm ground. Aladdin pleaded difficulty in climbing the steps, saying that the fruit that he had gathered heavily weighed him down.

Perceiving Aladdin's insolence, the Moor flew into a terrible rage and sprinkled more powder into the fire. As he muttered more magical words, the stone immediately moved back into its original place.

Feeling cheated by Aladdin from acquiring a wonderful treasure, and perceiving no other means to obtain what he sought, the magician took flight from China, making for his distant homeland.

Terrified, Aladdin screamed out from the dark place where he was confined. But it was to no avail. For two full days, he wept, unable to devise a means of fleeing from his entombment, save from calling upon the grace of Allah. Even the garden, with its blossoming trees and fine fruits, had been shut off from him.

In his desperation, Aladdin had all but forgotten that the man had given him a ring. In his anger, the man had also forgotten to retrieve this from Aladdin before beating his retreat. Without paying attention to it, at one point Aladdin found himself rubbing the ring, whereupon an enormous and frightful genie appeared before him. At once, the genie called aloud: "What do you ask of me, O master? I, slave of the ring, will obey your order!"

Aladdin commanded that he be set free from his prison. The genie conveyed him to safe ground in an instant, whereupon Aladdin made haste for his mother's home, swooning when he reached her door.

His mother embraced him, and then fetched food for him to eat, for he was very hungry after his long stay underground. Aladdin told his mother all that had happened, showing her the ring and the lamp that he had brought with him. Aladdin also showed his mother the fruit that he had gathered, which he now saw were really precious stones. It didn't surprise his mother to learn that the magician was no relative of the family's—this she had suspected when Aladdin first brought news of him.

When he had rested for a while, Aladdin asked his mother for more food. But she told him that there was none remaining in the house, for she had given him everything they had. She then promised to take her cotton wares to market, where she might raise sufficient coppers for them to afford some rice.

Aladdin proposed instead that his mother should sell the lamp that he had retrieved. His mother consented to his suggestion, but went first to clean the dusty object, such that it might fetch a better price at the souk. As she began to rub the lamp, there appeared in front of her a terrifying genie, who asked what command she would make of him.

Never having seen such an awful creature before, the poor woman screamed and—in great terror—fainted. However, emboldened by his recent adventure, Aladdin stood firm, seizing the lamp from his mother and boldly demanding: "Bring me food that I might eat!"

"I hear and obey!" replied the genie. In an instant, the slave of the lamp brought Aladdin a silver bowl and twelve silver plates, each filled with the choicest meats.

The genie also brought two silver goblets, and two flasks of luxuriant wine.

When his mother came to, she marvelled at what she saw laid out before her, questioning where the precious silverware and fine foods had come from. Aladdin told his mother first to eat, whereupon he told her about the genie and its magic.

"O, my son, have nothing to do with such evils!" implored his mother, "For this is forbidden by our great faith. If you do not heed my advice, the lamp will surely destroy you!"

The poor woman insisted that Aladdin sell the lamp, but he prevented her from taking it from him. "Destiny has brought the lamp into our hands," he argued, "And we must not forsake that which we have been given!"

Reluctantly, Aladdin's mother gave in to his demand to keep hold of the lamp, but warned that she would have nothing to do with it.

Aladdin made a small profit on each of the plates, which he sold to a dishonest jeweller, who paid him far less for each than they were worth. In time, Aladdin came to the truth of the trickster's ploy, when he happened to converse with an honest silversmith while on his way to the souk.

Thereafter, Aladdin sold the silverware at its proper value, calling favour on the genie to replenish his supply of plates whenever he exhausted his stock.

By this means, the small household was lifted out of poverty, and Aladdin and his mother never wanted for their supper.

During the course of his business, Aladdin learned that the emperor's daughter was soon to visit the baths in the city. He had heard that she was of the most stunning beauty, and he became obsessed with a desire to see her.

The emperor had commanded that every citizen must remain at home with their shutters closed while the princess enjoyed her visit. Aladdin was beside himself to catch a glimpse of the famous princess, even though to reveal himself in public would be to risk being punished with his life. He decided to run into the baths while no one was watching, and to hide behind one of the long drapes that hung there.

The princess, whose name was Badroulbadour, came to bathe as planned. From his spy's position, Aladdin was overcome with deep passion for her. Never before had he seen a woman undress–for until that time, he believed that all women were like his mother.

When the princess had departed, Aladdin stole away from the baths and made quickly for his home.

Certain that he was destined to be Badroulbadour's beloved, Aladdin told his mother what he had seen, imploring her to petition the emperor to grant him Badroulbadour's hand in marriage.

"Have you fully given leave to your senses?" screamed his mother. "By what presumption will the emperor entertain such a demand from a poor woman such as myself? Surely, this will bring shame upon our family, and may even risk our lives!"

Aladdin was unmoved by his mothers protest. He confidently predicted that the emperor would honour his request, and that were his mother not ready to show her love for him by making this petition, he would surely die from grief.

And so—full of fear—the troubled woman took several of the precious jewels that Aladdin had gathered in the orchard, and placed these in a basket, which she then covered with a kerchief. She then went to seek an audience with the emperor, who frequently held court in the city, at what was one of his favourite palaces in the land.

Joining the queue of citizens who sought judgements from the emperor, Aladdin's mother waited all day to be called before the royal presence. However, the time made available for audience with him soon elapsed, and so the humble seamstress returned to wait her turn the next day, hoping that she might then be able to make her appeal.

Her visits to the palace continued for some days, but without achieving her objective. Soon, the emperor observed her among those who waited to see him, noticing that she diligently returned to the same place each day. He motioned his chief advisor to ensure that the woman was brought before him when he again gave audience.

When she came before his throne, Aladdin's mother prostrated herself at the emperor's feet, begging forgiveness for the audacity and insanity of the request that she wished to proffer. Being benevolent in nature, the emperor granted her immunity from harm should she propose anything that might bring shame upon her. He further agreed to her request that he receive her in private, save for the attendance of his advisor.

"Your Great Majesty," began the woman, "I am but the poorest among your subjects, yet my love for my son is so great that I am obliged to present you with his request, which he has been incapable to be dissuaded from."

She proceeded to describe the circumstances by which Aladdin had come to see the princess, and spoke of his incurable passion for her. At last, deeply trembling, Aladdin's mother made known her son's wish that the emperor might grant him his daughter's hand in marriage. As an offering to show the earnestness of her request, she set before the emperor the fine jewels that she had brought with her.

On hearing the outrageous request, the emperor burst into laughter, but he was astonished to see the glittering stones that were presented to him. Duly, he took private counsel with his advisor on what response he should offer the pitiful woman.

The advisor whispered that no one but his own son could be wedded to the princess, since this was appropriate for their rank, and had been previously agreed by the emperor. He therefore advised that the emperor dismiss the woman as a mad fool.

However, the emperor questioned his advisor's true motive in offering this advice, and called forth the woman to inform her that he would grant Aladdin his wish—but only after three months had elapsed.

Unable to believe her wonderful fortune, Aladdin's mother rushed home to share the good news with her son. The two made a great celebration, and prepared to wait for the day when Aladdin would meet his bride.

Aladdin waited patiently. However, when barely two months had passed, his mother was surprised one morning to come upon a large crowd, who were gathering in the city centre. Enquiring as to the cause of the excitement, she was informed that the princess was to be married with the son of the emperor's chief advisor later that day.

Aladdin was distraught when his mother brought him this startling news, but he collected himself, and devised a plan that would bring him what he desired. Aladdin took hold of the lamp, which he then rubbed gently. Immediately the genie appeared, begging his master to tell him what he would have him do.

Aladdin replied as follows: "The emperor has broken his promise, marrying his daughter to his advisor's son. Once they have settled into their bed, I command you to bring the princess and her husband to me here this night."

"I hear and I obey!" replied the genie.

After midnight, the genie brought the newlyweds to Aladdin's house, with both lying in their bed. Obeying Aladdin's order, the genie then shut up the young man in the freezing back yard, promising to return just before daybreak to receive his master's further instruction.

Aladdin was thus left alone with the princess, whom he assured that he had no wish to harm. He crept into bed alongside her, but placed a sword between them to make clear their boundary.

Still, the princess was terrified, and she passed the most miserable night of her life. Her new husband was similarly unable to sleep, trembling with the cold, and being at a loss to comprehend what had happened. Aladdin, meantime, slept soundly.

The genie returned just before daybreak, and on Aladdin's command, carried the princess, her husband, and their bed back to their palace chamber.

Soon after sunrise, the emperor came to visit his daughter, to enquire how she had spent the night. The poor girl was stricken with fear, finding herself unable to speak a word to her father. The emperor was troubled by her refusal to answer his question, so he sent for his wife, to see whether she might have better success in obtaining an explanation.

"Why are you so troubled, my child?" asked the princess's mother. "Why will you not speak to your father? Pray, tell me, what causes you to be afraid?"

Recovering herself a little, the princess proceeded to tell her mother about the strange events that she'd experienced the previous night. Her mother concluded that she was describing a wild dream, but was concerned to see that her daughter was still trembling.

Aladdin ordered the genie to bring the princess and her bridegroom to him again the following night, and again the night after that.

Each morning following her strange transportation, the princess could not speak for shock when her father came to greet her. Becoming angry at what he perceived was her disobedience, the emperor at last threatened to cut off his daughter's head unless she would speak to him. Fearing his wrath, the princess then told her father what she had told her mother.

After hearing the strange tale, the emperor sent for his advisor, proposing that he questioned his own son on the matter. The advisor's son related that he had spent two miserable nights in the cold, and had been unable to sleep. He further said that he would rather die than pass one more night in the cold, and bade his mother to petition the emperor to divorce his daughter. Seeing that their marriage had begun with such unhappiness, the emperor agreed to this desperate solution.

అఠ

Three months passed since the emperor had heard the case presented by Aladdin's mother. Aladdin then enjoined his mother to once more seek an audience at the palace, where she might remind the emperor of his promise.

Until the poor widow again appeared in his great hall, the emperor had all but forgotten his promise to her. But seeing her once more, he was quickly reminded of her audacious request. Minded to consider her appeal, the emperor again sought counsel with his advisor. Still jealous with rage at the indignity that had been inflicted on his son, the advisor proposed that any suitor worthy of the emperor's daughter must be able to provide a dowry of great value–one that no ordinary man could equal.

The emperor then bade Aladdin's mother to draw near, whereupon he presented his decision: "A good emperor must honour his promise, and I will honour mine. However, your son must be able to provide for my daughter, and so he must bring me forty gold bowls, each filled with the finest jewels, and to be carried to me by forty splendidly attired slaves. Tell your son that I await his answer."

After hearing the emperor's demand, Aladdin's mother was full of despair, feeling certain that her son would be heartbroken by such an impossible demand. So it was with a very heavy heart that she brought the news to him.

"The emperor will have his wish," Aladdin responded, much to his mother's amazement. "And I would give much more for the love of his precious daughter!"

Aladdin then took the lamp, summoning the genie to put into practice what the emperor had demanded. Within a few moments, the genie had brought what was required. Taking further instruction, the genie made the slaves to proceed to the palace, each carrying with them a bowl of fine jewels. Aladdin's mother walked ahead of the party.

When they were given entry to the palace courtyard, the slaves and the widow fell to their knees, hailing and protesting their loyalty to the emperor. The emperor marvelled at what he saw, and delayed no longer in granting Aladdin's mother what her son most desired.

Aladdin then called upon the genie again, demanding that he bring him a tunic embroidered with the finest gold thread, along with twenty slaves to attend him. He instructed the genie to summon a horse whose majesty outshone the finest in the emperor's stables. He also ordered the genie to prepare a perfumed bath for him, and to cater well for his mother's every need. Finally, he commanded the genie to bring him purses filled with ten thousand golden coins.

The genie took no more than a moment to complete Aladdin's request. Aladdin then mounted the horse that was brought for him, and proceeded through the city, throwing gold coins to everyone he passed as he made his way toward the palace. The humble tailor's son was so immaculately dressed and groomed, that not even his childhood friends could recognise him.

When Aladdin arrived at the palace, the emperor immediately came out to greet him. The royal host offered to order his daughter's wedding that very day. However, Aladdin begged that he might first be allowed time to construct a palace that would be fitting for his bride, and sought the emperor's instruction as to where this might be sited.

The emperor proposed that the new palace be erected right opposite his own. Duly, Aladdin took his leave to make arrangements for its construction.

Aladdin retired home, where he took out the magic lamp, calling forth the genie. The slave to the lamp immediately presented himself to Aladdin, asking what service his master would ask of him.

Aladdin commanded that a magnificent palace be built on the site that the emperor had appointed for him. The grandiose building was to be made of marble, encrusted with gold relief and topped by an imposing dome, which itself was to rimmed with rubies, emeralds and sapphires. Around the central atrium, six tall windows were to be installed on each of the four quarters. All but one of these was to be framed by an intricate lattice, which was to be decorated with the most precious jewels that had ever been seen. The remaining window was to be left unfinished.

The genie set about the gargantuan task that Aladdin had set him, completing the whole enterprise within a single night. The next morning, Aladdin's mother, escorted by one hundred slaves, proceeded to the palace to request that she might escort the princess to meet her betrothed. The entourage made its way to the new palace, accompanied by joyous music and cheered on by an adoring crowd.

The princess was overcome with delight when she saw Aladdin, knowing at once that she had found her perfect match. For his part, Aladdin could barely contain his excitement to finally meet the princess whose beauty had won his heart so many months before. So suited were they, that their wedding was arranged without further delay.

The sudden appearance of the magnificent palace astounded everyone. The emperor's jealous advisor suspected that sorcery must be responsible for such a marvellous happening. But the emperor would hear none of his complaint.

On visiting the palace, the emperor marvelled at its immaculate construction and luxurious decoration, but he questioned why a small part of one window had been left unfinished.

"This, Your Majesty, is deliberate," explained his host. "If it pleases Your Majesty, I would wish for this window to be finished with the handiwork of your own craftsmen."

The emperor was delighted to accept Aladdin's invitation, and commissioned his finest glaziers, jewellers, and stonemasons to set about the task. Soon, the artisans had laid claim to the finest jewels that the Treasury contained–such was the impossibility of complementing the immaculate work that had been wrought by the genie. But after six months of labour, the window remained incomplete.

Duly, Aladdin proposed that the craftsmen give up their task, and return the jewels that they'd taken from the Treasury. Thereafter, the lattice was soon completed under Aladdin's command of the slave of the lamp.

This gesture convinced the emperor's advisor that Aladdin must be engaged in a malevolent practice, but the emperor's increasing impatience with his suspicion made him wary of pressing his case further.

During the period since his betrothal to the princess, Aladdin had earned great popularity among the people of the city. He became well known for his generosity to the poor, and became greatly esteemed for the courteous manner with which he conducted himself. As son-in-law to the emperor and often acting in his stead, he had led armies to several famous victories in battle.

❧

Meanwhile, many miles away, an old man was casting spells and divining truths with his magic. This was none other than the wicked magician who had earlier left Aladdin to die in the cave of treasure.

Through his sorcery, the Moor discovered that Aladdin had escaped from the cave and was now son-in-law to the emperor. By the same means, the magician learned that the boy whom he'd assumed as his nephew was now living in a magnificent palace in the very city where he had first found him.

Feeling certain that a tailor's son could only come upon such fortune through the power of the lamp, the outraged magician resolved to use any means to gain possession of the lamp for himself. Crossing many deserts, and traversing many mountain passes, the Moor came at last to the city that he'd visited many months before.

When he arrived in the city, the magician asked where he might see the magnificent palace that had come to be known abroad as a wonder of the world. Confirming that he had found the right place, and also learning that Aladdin was then away from the city on a hunting expedition, the Moor set about the next stage of his plan.

Firstly, he purchased twelve sparkling new lamps, which he gathered into a basket. Then he disguised himself as a street merchant, positioned himself close by the walls of Aladdin's palace, and then began calling out to passers-by, "New lamps for old! New lamps for old!"

Before long, a loud commotion broke out, as more and more people gathered to hear his absurd cry. "Who is this?" teased many in the crowd, "Who offers new lamps for old!" Soon, the magician's cries were drowned out by the loud guffaws and raucous jeering of the throng.

Hearing the commotion outside the palace, the princess sent one of her slaves to discover what had excited the crowd. The slave returned with the explanation, even breaking into laughter herself when telling of the crazy man's business.

The slave proposed that the princess silence the man by offering him an old lamp that she had seen kept in a niche in the grand hall of the palace–this being the very lamp that had afforded Aladdin his fortune. Perceiving the lamp to have no value, the princess agreed to the slave's proposal. And so, a deal was struck with the magician, who thus secured the great treasure that he coveted.

Still suffering the taunts of the crowd, the Moor departed from the city, coming to a place where others could no longer see him. Here, he reached for the lamp and called forth the genie.

"I am the slave of the lamp!" said the genie. "What, O Master, do you ask of me?"

"Bring me, the princess and the palace where she resides to my homeland in North Africa!" ordered the Moor. No sooner had he uttered these words, than the genie completed his command. In an instant, nothing remained where the mighty palace had once stood.

After sunrise, the emperor looked out from his chamber window and was astonished to see that the magnificent palace that Aladdin had erected was gone. Thinking that he might not yet have come to his senses, the grand ruler called for his advisor, to tell him what he made of the matter. The advisor saw too that the palace had vanished, and felt certain that the only reason could be sorcery.

Having rejected his advisor's allegations for so long, the emperor was now finally convinced that Aladdin had used enchantment to create the palace, and that he'd employed the same method to make it disappear. He at once commanded thirty soldiers from his elite guard to go quickly to the forest where Aladdin's hunting party had made its camp, ordering them to bring his son-in-law back to him in chains.

The emperor's guards did as they were commanded, though they were deeply saddened to parade Aladdin in this way, since they dearly loved him. As he was dragged through the city on the way back to the palace, many citizens cried out for him, for they too had come to greatly admire the generous, gracious and charming tailor's son.

When he was brought into the palace courtyard, the emperor immediately called for his executioner, refusing to give audience to Aladdin. The executioner made the prisoner fall to his knees, then bandaged his eyes. Just as the executioner had raised his scimitar, ready to slay the perceived trickster, the emperor's advisor noticed a large crowd that was making for the palace. Some of their number had already scaled its outer walls, and appeared ready to riot.

Angry voices called for the sparing of Aladdin's life, hailing him as a peaceable and worthy member of the royal household.

Fearing the crowd's rage, the emperor ordered his executioner to steady his hand. Aladdin was released from his bondage, and was at last able to speak.

"My Glorious Majesty, why have you brought me here in this manner?" questioned Aladdin. "I cannot see, Sir, that I have done you any wrong."

"Then perhaps you might explain where the palace of yours has gone, and what has become of my daughter?" hollered the emperor. "The removal of your palace I can entertain, but the loss of my daughter–and your sorcery–I cannot!"

Aladdin was astonished when he saw that his palace had indeed disappeared. He could summon no explanation for what had happened, but begged the emperor to allow him time to find his daughter.

"You have forty days to bring my daughter home," roared the emperor. "If you do not return with the one who is most precious to me within this time, your head will not be spared the sword a second time!"

Aladdin departed from the emperor's company, desperate to know how he might discover the whereabouts of his dear wife. For several days, he wandered the streets like a vagabond, delirious and uncertain what he should do. Others sympathised with him, but could not offer him counsel.

Aladdin began to walk away from the city, coming upon a river. Crouching beside the fast-flowing stream, he at one point thought that he might throw himself into its path and be done with everything. In his agitated state, he didn't notice that he had nervously rubbed the ring that the magician had given to him before charging him to fetch the lamp. Aladdin had quite forgotten that he was still wearing this very ring.

At once, a genie appeared before him, asking what service Aladdin would have him perform.

"Bring me back my palace, my princess, and save my life!" Aladdin replied.

"My master, this I cannot do!" answered the genie in a troubled voice. "This gift lies only under the command of the genie of the lamp."

Aladdin reflected on his dilemma for a moment, and then instructed: "Bring me to the place where I can find my wife." This request was within the genie's power to command, and so Aladdin was carried to a resting place beside his palace, which now stood in a desolate land in North Africa.

Exhausted from his experience, and now seeing nighttime approaching, Aladdin sat down beside one of the apartments of the palace. He soon fell into a deep sleep.

❧❧

Meantime, since she had been transported to this hostile land, the princess had refused the advances of the magician. She pined for her homeland, and refused to believe the Moor's claim that the emperor had killed Aladdin. Such was her disdain for the African, that she refused to dine with him, and she kept a separate quarter in the palace.

On the morning following Aladdin's flight from China, the princess awoke earlier than was her habit. She was astonished to see her husband lying outside her apartment, and immediately commanded one of her slaves to awaken him and bring him to her.

After hearing her story and learning of her miserable life with the Moor, Aladdin realised that the magician had used his cunning to gain possession of the lamp, with which he had been able to command the genie to bring the palace and the princess to his own land.

"My darling wife, pray tell me whether or not you have seen an old lamp about this place—one that used to be found in a niche of the hall of many windows?" pleaded Aladdin.

"Yes, my dear husband," the princess replied. "The magician once showed it to me, but he keeps it hidden about his person so that no one can take it from him."

Aladdin pondered the situation, and then decided upon a plan. He journeyed to the nearest town, where he purchased a small quantity of a rare powder. At the market there, he bought a new suit of clothes to disguise himself with, lest the magician notice him walking by the palace.

Having returned to the princess's quarters, Aladdin handed her the powder that he had bought, then told her his plan.

"My dear, while you will find this hard, here is what you must do," he began. "Call the Moor to you this evening, and tell him that you have carefully considered what he has told you. Say that you now recognise that his claims must be true, and that you long to enjoy his company. Invite him to sup with you, so that you might celebrate your coming together. Flatter him by choosing wines from his country rather than from our own, and tell him that you have no desire to return to China."

Aladdin went on to explain that the powder would immediately cause anyone who consumed it to become senseless. This was to be sprinkled into the goblet set at the princess's place. Once the wine had been served, the princess should offer her cup in exchange for the Moor's–a custom that symbolised the sealing of a union.

Aladdin then retired from his wife's apartment, and the pair waited for evening, when the plan could be put into action.

The magician was easily persuaded by the princess's charms, and was taken in by her story of her change of heart. They passed their goblets–exchanging one with the other–and after some cheerful conversation, raised their glasses to toast each other. They then drank from the wine.

At once, the magician fell back in his seat, as though dead. Aladdin then crept into the room from behind a curtain where he had been hiding, drawing a blade from an inner pocket of his garment. Without hesitation, Aladdin plunged the knife into the belly of the man who had cheated him, bringing his treachery to an end.

Aladdin then reached inside the Moor's cape, where he found the magic lamp. Summoning the genie to appear, he then commanded that the palace and all who were in it be immediately transported back to its original place.

Meanwhile, the emperor continued to mourn the loss of his daughter. Such was his grief, that he thought that his senses were deceiving him. So it was when, rubbing his eyes, he suddenly saw Aladdin's magnificent palace once more standing opposite his own.

The emperor sent quickly for his daughter, and also for Aladdin. They told him all that had happened– that the palace had been carried away by the wish of an evil magician, whose dead body they were able to show. Hearing how cruelly his daughter had been treated, and lamenting that he had ever doubted Aladdin's integrity, the emperor ordered a week-long festival to celebrate their return.

All might have been well for the happy couple, but this was not to be.

෨ఌఞ

It happened that the magician had a brother, whose cunning and designs were even more wicked than his own. Divining what had happened through his sorcery, the man came to Aladdin's city, where he resolved to avenge his brother's death.

Arriving in the city, the evil one soon learned that there was a holy woman who was well known there—who went by the name of Fatima. This woman frequently left her hermitage to come to the city, where she would offer prayers and give blessings for the sick and needy. This woman had earned a famous reputation for her compassion and ability to heal many ailments.

Discovering the location of the holy woman's retreat, the magician's brother came to her, quickly taking a knife to her throat. He then put on her dress and veil, so as to portray her appearance and convince others that she was still alive. Wearing this disguise, he came close by Aladdin's palace to offer prayers to anyone who might come to him.

Hearing the crowd's excitement that this appearance gave rise to, the princess instructed one of her slaves to bring the woman to her, whose humility and purity she had often heard about.

The false healer was duly brought before the princess, and was then invited to spend time with her, while Aladdin was away on a hunting expedition.

The supposed ascetic marvelled at the elaborate furnishings of the palace, but proposed that the great hall of windows lacked one thing—a roc's egg[13], sus-

---

[13] A roc is a legendary giant bird of prey, famously referred to in the tales of *Sinbad the Sailor*.

pended from the dome, like a mighty chandelier. This, the trickster said, would truly make the palace the greatest wonder in the world.

Convinced of the wisdom of this suggestion, the princess began to think of nothing else. When Aladdin return from his hunt, the princess quickly made known her desire for a roc's egg to be installed in the palace. Aladdin agreed, and called forth the genie of the lamp, whom he ordered to bring the princess's wish to fruition.

However, rather than obey his master's command, the genie flew into a wild temper–his voice trembling so loudly that the very ground below began to shake.

"Willingly I have obeyed your every command!" bellowed the genie. "A fine palace I have built for you, and I rescued you from the desert. Now you ask that I profane the honour of my own mother! For this, you deserve to be burned to ashes! But know that it is not you who really makes this command, but the will of an evildoer who has put this idea into the princess's head!"

The genie proceeded to explain that the magician's brother had used deceit to gain the princess's confidence, and was still dwelling at her pleasure within the palace, disguised as an old healer.

After hearing the genie's warning, Aladdin came to his wife, complaining that he had a headache. "Might this holy woman that I have heard about bring me comfort?" he asked.

"Certainly, my dear husband," the princess replied, then instructing one of her slaves to bring the one whom she perceived to be Fatima to her.

Aladdin explained his need, and knelt down to receive the wicked imposter's blessing. But without allowing time for chants or a touching of hands, Aladdin drew out a blade that he had hidden about his person, plunging the shining steel into the heart of the deceiver.

"O my husband, have you gone quite mad!" cried the princess. "Why have you taken anger on this most holy of women?"

Aladdin then explained what the genie had told him, and his wife loved him all the more for his faithfulness.

In time, the emperor passed away, and Aladdin succeeded him. Aladdin became a very popular and celebrated leader, and through his blood, headed a long line of kings.

What am I bid?

Before I reached my sixteenth birthday, I'd rarely ventured beyond the boundaries of Tai Po—the sprawling community in the New Territories of Hong Kong that had been my home for most of my life. My father had owned a small house in a village on the edge of the district, but had needed to sell this in order to pay off a business debt. His grocery business in downtown Kowloon never made much money, although it's still a mystery to me why he always had so little to feed my mother and I.

As an only child, father was keen for me to make a better success of my career than had he. Before he died in a road accident, he made arrangements for me to train to be an electrician when I left school.

The prospect of spending my days wiring up electric systems never excited me. When I finished my studies, I wanted to enjoy myself, before having to concern myself with settling down into some mundane job. Mother used to deride me for what she saw as my laziness, constantly badgering me to bring in some money, which was desperately needed to complement her meagre income earned from her work at a restaurant.

It's true that I spent many hours on my Xbox, and found it hard to resist getting involved in what I know were aimless conversations on Facebook. Many of my mates were doing the same–excepting those who'd decided to make a go of their education.

I had had a couple of jobs–cleaning cars, delivering flyers, and pestering people to take part in some survey or another for a market research firm that paid me according to how many questionnaires I collected. But these never promised permanent work, and most of the money that I earned was spent on trips to burger bars and coffee shops.

One opportunity to earn a few extra dollars came up when a friend of mine told me that his dad was looking for someone to help out with a move. I couldn't understand why he thought that I might be suitable for the job, since I had little muscle on me–being barely able to lift a sack of carrots. But I was easily persuaded to volunteer my services at the promise of receiving the princely sum of ten thousand dollars for my trouble.

"You won't have to do much, Ken," my friend assured me. "Just do what my old fellah asks, and the job will be over in a jiffy!"

I told my mother about the suggestion, but she was dubious about the motives of my friend's dad. "You need to be wary of that Lam family," she warned me. "And why on earth are they planning to move house overnight?"

It was true that I'd been asked to meet my friend's father at an address on Hong Kong Island late the following evening, but I assumed that loading the removals vehicle would be easier at night than during the desperate chaos of the day.

In the event, no house move was planned. Mr. Lam and three other muscular gentleman led me down a service alley that ran behind a block of shops on Cat Street—one of the main antique trading areas in the Central district of Hong Kong Island.

We ascended a fire escape to reach the flat roof of the backroom of one of the shops. The backrooms on this particular block extended to only one storey, although the front-facing structure reached to five or six levels.

With a skill that I assumed must have been professionally gained, one of the men scored a groove into the square pane of one half of a window that served as a skylight for the building. He expertly cut through the glass without making a sound–a feat that was all the more impressive since his thick fingers were enveloped by the taut fabric of a leather glove.

My friend's dad and the other man watched impassively. I had no option than to join them, since they had blocked my access to the galvanized steel staircase of the fire escape. When the glass panel had been carefully lifted out of its frame, my friend's dad crouched beside me to explain my part in the enterprise.

"Sorry we had to bring you here under false pretences, young Ken," he whispered, "But this is a delicate mission." I was beginning to realise that I had got myself into a difficult situation, but I didn't anticipate what he wanted me to do next.

"We want you to help us with our move–to move a little item out of the care of our shopkeeper friend below. "Fingers Lo" here will help you get fitted with a harness, and then we'll gently lower you through the hole. You'll need to take this head torch with you, as we're going to interrupt the electricity supply to disable the alarm."

My trustless employer went on to describe the item that I was to recover. "When you've freed yourself from the harness in the backroom, go toward the door that's opposite the wall on which you'll see hanging a mahogany carving of a fighting dragon. There you'll see a small cupboard at about you shoulder height, which is where our friend keeps the keys to his cabinets. Take the set of keys that you'll find hanging on the third peg from your left, one of which will allow you to unlock the door and go through into the shop.

"To your left, you'll see a chest of three drawers, about a metre wide. One of the keys on the set that you take from the cupboard will open the middle drawer of the chest. Open this, then look for a golden amulet, engraved with an inscription requesting the support of *Lao Zi*.

"Waste no time in putting this in your pocket, then re-secure the door, retrace your steps into the back-room—locking the door behind you—and return the keys to the place where you found them. Then place the harness around you once more, and tug on the rope to inform us that you're ready to come out. One thousand crisp ten dollar notes will be waiting for you here!"

It was clear why Mr. Lam wanted someone of my proportions to help him recover the talisman—anyone who carried more weight wouldn't be able to squeeze through the hole in the skylight. I felt very unsure about what I was being asked to do, but was strangely excited at the same time—and I'd already made up my mind about how I was going to spend the ten thousand dollars.

I therefore offered no objection as "Fingers" helped secure me into the harness, then I gripped hold of the rope, and was slowly lowered to the floor. The room that I found myself in was exactly as Mr. Lam had described it. I quickly located the set of keys that would give me access to the shop, and within a moment, had located the charm that I'd been instructed to fetch, placing it in my pocket.

I waited a moment to catch my breath, my adrenaline rushing through my body. I felt strangely excited by my daring, even though I realized the wrongdoing that I was committing. As my heartbeat slowed to a normal level, I suddenly had a strong impression that I shouldn't retrace my path to the men on the roof. I hesitated, starting toward the backroom, but my conviction that I should stay where I was grew stronger with every hesitant step.

After a time, I heard Mr. Lam calling me, keeping his voice low to avoid attracting attention, but still loud enough for me to hear.

"Ken, what are you doing down there?" he cried. "Get out immediately–we've got to go. Immediately!"

I hid myself in a corner of the shop, hoping that Mr. Lam wouldn't be able to see me if he peered into the hole. I could already hear a police siren wailing in the background, which I felt certain must be destined for our neighbourhood. I reasoned that someone must have caught sight of the little gathering on the roof, and then alerted the police. Now I felt certain that I was in trouble, whichever way I turned.

Not hearing their voices any more, I assumed that my fellow accomplices had made a speedy exit. I had been right to believe that the police were beating a fast path for the shop.

I heard the footsteps of several officers scrambling on the roof. Carefully shuffling from my hiding place to peer through the door into the backroom, I could just glimpse the gleaming steel of three submachine gun barrels peeking through the hole, which were trained on different parts of the room.

The bright blue light of the several cars that had arrived outside easily filtered through the shop's shutters, but there was no obvious movement among the gathered officers. It seems that the police had waited for the owner of the shop to arrive, whom they'd alerted to the break-in. It was then that their silence was broken with a clear message that was barked through a megaphone:

"Police! You're surrounded! Put down your weapons, and reveal yourself!"

Shaking, I raised my hands and walked slowly into the backroom.

"I'm alone!" I shouted. "I'm unarmed. Honestly, I'm alone!"

I could hear muffled conversation above me, and was able to pick up on some of the words that were coming across on the radio to the men on the roof–I imagined from officers on the ground.

"It's just one kid, Sir!" said one of the men on the roof. "We've got infra on the building, and aren't picking up any more heat. We're fixed on the kid, and he's unarmed. Propose ground entry."

I overheard an indistinct exchange on the radio, amid what sounded like other voices, and then heard the locks of the shop door being opened.

"Stay where you are, keeping your hands up!" barked one of the officers who rushed into the building from the front. Others had entered from the rear, while the gun barrels above stayed firmly aimed at me.

I could say nothing. It was clear to the small army that had crowded into the shop that I had no intention of offering any resistance. I was handcuffed and led into a waiting van.

At the police station I was treated respectfully, but was left without any doubt that my interviewer wanted answers to her questions.

"Who was with you?" I was repeatedly asked. "Who put you up to this?"

At first, I struggled to find my voice, not knowing what I should say. If I betrayed Mr. Lam, he would surely come looking for me. But my mum was less likely to hold her silence were she questioned about my whereabouts. Despite fearing what Mr. Lam might do to me, I had a strong feeling that I should tell the truth.

I told the inspector everything I knew about the planned robbery–how I'd been asked to help with what I thought was meant to be a house move, how I'd been trapped by the men on top of the roof, and how I'd felt uneasy about returning to the roof when I'd taken the charm from the drawer.

I was left alone in a cell for several hours, but it seemed that I'd said enough to convince the police that my story was genuine. The door to my cell was eventually opened, and my mother was shown in.

She ran toward me and hugged me like she used to when I was only a few feet high. Right at that moment, I felt just as small–putting my trust in my mother's arms.

Once some paperwork had been completed, I was told that I would not face any charges, and was free to go.

The amulet that I had stolen was returned to its rightful owner, who I discovered was a goat-bearded man in his 60's called Mr. Tam.

I spent the following days close to home, but having assured my mother that I wouldn't go anywhere near Mr. Lam again, she felt able to allow me to roam freely again. As it happened, Mr. Lam and his associates had disappeared–presumably realising that I may have disclosed their identity when the police picked me up.

I was afraid that they would come looking for me, but could see that I had no option than to carry on with my normal life. I had nowhere to stay other than in my mother's apartment, and I couldn't leave her alone while Lam and his cronies were still on the run.

Despite knowing that he might want to scold me, I had a strong feeling that I must make a visit to Mr. Tam's shop in Cat Street. I told my mother what I planned to do, explaining that I felt compelled to offer the distressed shopkeeper my personal apology.

As I made my way downtown, my stomach churned as I contemplated how Mr. Tam might receive me. The ten minute crossing on the Star Ferry between Tsim Sha Tsui and Central had never seemed so fast, bringing me closer as it did to the place where I must face my reckoning.

Mr. Tam was serving a customer when I walked into his shop. As he was completing the sale, he passed a wary glance at me, although I wasn't sure he recognised who I was. He had only seen me briefly when I was led from his shop in handcuffs into the police van.

I nervously waited for Mr. Tam to finish his transaction, then taking a deep breath and clenching my fists to anchor myself, I proceeded to introduce myself, explaining my reason for visiting.

The unruffled shopkeeper listened without interruption. Then, after a thoughtful pause, he gave his response: "I accept your apology, young man. You have taken courage to come here, and from what I understand, your breaking into my shop was not something that you'd premeditated."

I bowed in gratitude before the gracious gentleman, before he continued: "Your honesty with the police, and your readiness to apologise impress me. I'm looking for a little extra help to run the shop at the moment, and wonder whether you might consider working for me?"

Mr. Tam's offer was furthest from the outcomes that I'd imagined before making my apology. I eagerly accepted his proposal, and soon found myself becoming acquainted with the world of antiques and rare treasures.

My enthusiasm to learn impressed Mr. Tam, and soon he invited me to join him on a buying mission to the giant flea market in Shenzhen. He taught me the art of negotiation, and shared some of the knowledge that he'd built up over his many years of bargain hunting.

Most of what we bought was left with a transporter in Shenzhen, who then delivered the goods to Mr. Tam's premises in Cat Street some days later. I never learned what route these took across the border from the mainland, but I thought it best not to ask.

I learned the business quickly, and Mr. Tam was pleased with my progress. I even started a night class to learn about Chinese porcelain marks, which helped me become better able to sort out what was real from what was fake. Soon, I began making recommendations about what we might buy, and Mr. Tam rewarded me with a share of the profits on the more lucrative items that I discovered.

I'd asked Mr. Tam about the amulet that the thieves had wanted me to procure for them. He explained that it had little material value to him, but was regarded as something of a trophy that had been captured from a "rival", and then presented to him for safekeeping. The charm had since been given to him. I didn't then know what he meant by this, but would later find out.

Mr. Tam said that the charm was meant to bring its bearer good luck, but he had yet to benefit from its supposed power. Reflecting on the incident that had nearly landed me in serious trouble, he suggested that I might like to have it. I was overwhelmed to receive this small but mesmerizing object, and vowed never to be separated from it.

托托

Mr. Leung, a regular visitor to the shop, was a well-known property tycoon, who lived in a smart apartment on The Peak. Along with his chauffeur, he was often accompanied by a strikingly beautiful young woman, who Mr. Lam told me was his daughter.

I looked forward to their visits, since I could barely stop thinking about this amazing lady's beauty. She was rarely separated from her father, but on one occasion when he was busily engaged in a negotiation with Mr. Lam, I took my chance to ask her if she would join me for a date.

I don't know how I suddenly summoned the confidence to make such a forthright suggestion to a girl that I'd never spoken to before. However, to my surprise and delight, she passed me her business card, and asked me to call her later that day.

I learned that this beautiful lady's name was Po Yi, and that she was the only daughter of her jealous father. He was very protective toward her, and wary of any man that sought to befriend her. She said that her father would be travelling to the mainland the following week, and proposed that this would give us an opportunity to meet.

The days before Po Yi and I came together at the Lei Garden restaurant on Kowloon Bay could not pass quickly enough. I made all manner of plans about what I would say to her when we met, but in the event, she wasted no time in telling me that she'd felt drawn to me since she first saw me in the shop. Only when her father was away did she have an opportunity to break free from the family home.

Po Yi and I began to meet regularly after then—whenever she was able to slip away from her father's attention. We knew that our backgrounds meant that our parents would see us as unsuitable soulmates–she being the daughter of a powerbroker of repute, and me from a marginalized class. However, eventually we both felt that the time had arrived to declare our love before our families.

My mother was shocked by the revelation, but held back her reservation–offering us her blessing. "You've come a long way since you began at the shop," she told me, "You're no longer my small boy!"

Mr. Leung was much less gracious, although his wife stated that her first wish was for her daughter's happiness.

"How can you even think about dating a boy from the villages?" Mr. Leung demanded of his daughter. "No man is worthy of my daughter's recognition unless he's of suitable standing!"

"How do you think that a pathetic wretch like that shop assistant can provide the life for you that you deserve?" he went on. "Where do you think you're going to live?"

Po Yi pleaded with her father to allow her to continue seeing me, but he was adamant that if she wished for him to consider her his daughter, she must obey his wishes.

We met briefly only one more time after Po Yi was presented with this ultimatum. As we walked hand-in-hand by the harbour, she told me that her father had decided to take her to his second home in Shanghai, and that he'd demanded that she change her cell phone number and online contact details.

While I felt close to tears, I kissed her, and promised that our love would endure whatever her father
thought about us. Po Yi was painfully unhappy, but for
now, she felt that she had no option than to comply
with her father's wishes.

I grieved desperately for Po Yi after she moved out
of the family apartment the following week. As she'd
warned me, her cell phone number was changed, and I
found that I could no longer reach her by email or
Facebook.

My mother tried to console me, telling me that I
would soon find new love and that my parting from Po
Yi was for the best, given our differing social backgrounds. Of course, I didn't believe her.

❧

After Po Yi left for Shanghai, something that did
distract my attention for a while was an article in the
newspaper that I read on my way to work.

"GANG BOSS SHOT DEAD IN CASINO CAR
PARK," ran the headline in the *South China Morning
Post.* "Man Ki Lam, well known to police as a leading
member of the 14K, was killed in cold blood as he left
the *Rio* hotel and casino in Macau late last night," the
report went on. "Lam–aka *Smiley Face*–had been on
the run since leading an attempted break-in at the
Lucky Tam's antique mart in Central. He is believed to
have been hunted down by members of rival gang Sun
Yee On."

I couldn't believe the news. I hadn't imagined that Mr. Lam was involved in such a renowned outfit. But the news begged an important question for me—was my own trusted employer also associated with a criminal cooperative?

When I arrived at the shop that morning, I was wary about mentioning the story to Mr. Tam. But he must have noticed my abnormal aloofness, rightly suspecting that I'd read the news about the shooting in Macau.

"I'm not a member of Sun Yee On," he informed me, "I've never acted against the law either. But I do need to pay money to them," he continued. "They say that it's for my own protection—having all these valuable vases and silverware on display needs someone to keep a lookout for any suspicious goings-on."

"So where was your minder when Lam forced me to break open the lock on your drawer?" I asked. Mr. Tam responded with a solemn stare, making it clear that I shouldn't expect an answer.

I reasoned that it might be dangerous for him to say too much, and so I resisted asking further questions.

My trading continued to go well. Mr. Tam was now happy for me to pay visits alone to the flea market in Shenzhen. I had a talent for spotting valuable items, and had become accomplished at striking a hard bargain. I always kept the amulet with me, which I felt sure helped draw me to the fabulous treasures that I acquired for the shop. Mr. Tam was happy for me to buy items for myself and have them brought back to the shop by his transporter, provided these were paid for with my own money.

Po Yi was never far from my thoughts. I was unable to think about even talking to another girl, and I longed to know how my lover was faring in her new home, many miles to the north. I was determined to save hard, to prove to her father–if I could get to speak with him–that I could be more than a perfect match for his daughter.

As I lay awake each night thinking about my darling, I tried to fathom how I could ever earn enough money to impress Mr. Leung. I trusted that the amulet would help me, and began to ask the spirit that possessed it to show me a way for being reunited with my lover.

Trusting the feelings that came when I opened my heart in this way, I developed a strong sense that I should pay a visit to a particular stall at the flea market when I next made a journey across the border.

Following this lead, I was astonished to discover a dirty wine cup that was hidden under a torn napkin. While I could not immediately be sure of its provenance, I recognised that the object might be a rare treasure from the Ming Dynasty–a find that could fetch many hundreds of thousands of dollars at auction.

No one else appeared to have noticed the cup, and the stallholder had no concept of its possible value. I concluded a deal with him for only fifty Yuan, then carefully packaged my purchase, ready to be brought back to the shop by Mr. Tam's transporter.

When I returned to the shop, I described my find to Mr. Tam. He seemed very interested to hear about what I might have discovered, giving me his assurance that whatever its value–since it had been bought with my own money–it was mine.

When the package arrived and Mr. Tam examined its marks with his practiced eye, he felt certain that I might have laid my hands on a real treasure. He recommended that I take the cup to Christie's auction house, whose experts would be able to confirm its authenticity.

I followed Mr. Tam's advice, and waited impatiently for Christie's response. The cup proved to be far rarer than I'd imagined–I was advised to put it up for auction with a minimum reserve of no less than $3 million. If the cup sold, I would receive a bounty far beyond what I'd ever dreamed.

The item appeared in Christies' September catalogue of *Rare items from the Ming Dynasty*. On the day of the auction, I took my seat at the back of the hall a little before the bidding began.

"Lot 103. Rare wine cup from the Ming Dynasty. Mint condition, with cockerel and chicken decoration," the auctioneer began. "What am I bid? Who will start me with $1 million?"

A man close to the front who I couldn't make out quickly raised his paddle. "Two million?" the auctioneer came back quickly. A paddle went up on the other side of the room. "Three million? Do I see three million?" The gentleman who'd been first to bid raised his paddle once more. "Four million? Who will offer me four million? One exceptional item, rarely seen at auction," the auctioneer returned.

A bid came in from a phone bidder, and the auctioneer raised the stake to $5 million. I was barely able to contain my excitement at this point, but there was a seemingly never-ending period of hesitation among the bidders, before the gentleman at the front once again raised his paddle.

"Five-Five?" Came back the auctioneer, hinting at a price that might achieve the winning bid. "Five-Five— Do I hear Five-Five?" Another unending silence, then an offer was taken from a phone bidder. "Six million?" ventured the auctioneer. "Will anyone offer me $6 million?" The auctioneer scanned the room, holding open the offer until he was sure that no one was tempted to tender. But the man at the front shook his head, and so the hammer came down at five and a half million dollars.

I ran out of the room and screamed! The cup had fetched nearly twice its reserve price, and I was now a rich man! In my excitement, I barely noticed a man walking up to me, offering to shake my hand.

"Congratulations!" he beamed. After regaining my senses, I could see that the hand that I was shaking was that of my old friend, Mr. Tam.

"For a moment then, I thought that I'd pushed things too far!" he went on. "I never meant to go to five million, but I felt that it was worth one further push!"

"You mean that you were the man bidding at the front?" I enquired, struggling to come to terms with what I'd heard.

Mr. Tam nodded, his growing smile breaking his normally unassuming composure. "I thought that I'd do my little bit to help move things along," he revealed. "If the hammer had come down at five million, I would have had to shut down the shop. But I know how much you want to impress the father of that girl of yours!"

I couldn't help tears from forming in my eyes, and I instinctively found myself embracing the man who'd shown me kindness since the first time I'd met him.

"I will share the profit with you!" I promised. "Without your help, I would never have made it here!"

However, Mr. Tam was adamant that he didn't want a share of my earnings, saying that he felt sure that the amulet had played no small part in bringing me the success that he said I deserved.

I too felt that I had the amulet to thank, and so I was diligent in expressing my gratitude to the spirit of the charm. At the same time, I couldn't prevent myself from making one further request for its assistance– that I could cross paths again with Mr. Leung, and impress him sufficiently for him to bless my friendship with his daughter.

I held the amulet close to my heart, waiting for inspiration. What came to me could not have been a product of my imagination. I felt that I was to order a fine-tailored silk wool suit for myself, to purchase an exclusive Patek Philippe watch, and then to hire a Mercedes S-class and chauffeur to cruise around the hallowed streets of The Peak. If fortune smiled on me, and I caught sight of Mr. Leung leaving his house in his Jaguar XJ, I was to instruct my driver to follow him.

The plan seemed like an act of fantasy, but I knew that I should always trust what the amulet led me to do. I had a strong feeling that I should bide my time, waiting a full two months before acting on the plan. When my suit was ready, and I'd given up some of my auction profit to buy myself a stunning Patek Philippe watch, I waited a further four weeks before arranging my expensive car hire.

My chauffeur drove me to the corner of the street where Mr. Leung lived, where we waited for several hours. Finally, the tall gates in front of his apartment block swung open and his silver XJ came into view. "This is the one!" I motioned to my driver. "Follow that car!"

We kept close to the tail of the Jaguar as we descended The Peak, but were separated at traffic signals as we levelled out toward the waterfront. My driver was quick to overtake other traffic, and soon we were riding close to Mr. Leung's bumper once more.

The XJ came to a stop outside the distinctive tower of the headquarters of the Hong Kong and Shanghai Bank. Mr. Leung's chauffeur stepped out the vehicle, to open the door for Mr. Leung. I'd already alighted onto the street, and made a steady path toward Mr. Leung.

"Mr. Leung!" I shouted. "Fancy meeting you here! Do you remember me–the joker that you thought wasn't good enough for your daughter?"

"What are you doing here?" Mr. Leung abruptly replied. "Can't you see that I'm busy?"

"I'm in a hurry too," I retorted, purposefully checking my watch to make sure that Mr. Leung could see the expensive wrist-gear that I was wearing. "My chauffeur is parked on a yellow line, and I've an appointment with my account manager at the bank!"

Mr. Leung looked disbelievingly as I pointed to the Mercedes that was parked close behind him, then seemed to be in shock as he let his eyes explore the full profile of my immaculately tailored suit.

"I've made quite a few million since we last met," I offered–answering the question that I was sure was preoccupying Mr. Leung's mind. "If it weren't for my love for Po Yi, I would never have made that my goal."

Mr. Leung seemed unsure what he should say to me, but he didn't want to engage in a lengthy conversation at that moment.

"Might you consider allowing your daughter to see me?" I asked, as Mr. Leung started to walk toward the revolving door of the imposing building.

"We'll see," was his only response, as he took one last astonished glance at me, and then made his way into the bank.

I didn't know if this brief encounter would be enough to win him over. Still, I trusted the guidance that had come to me when I'd asked for the amulet's assistance.

∂∘∾

Five days later I received a phone call from Po Yi. Her father had informed her about his meeting with me, and had said that after reflection, he felt that it might be acceptable for us to meet again. Po Yi was due to fly back to Hong Kong the following week, and was eager to know when we might meet.

I promised to take her to the *Lookout* restaurant on The Peak, and assured her that no one other than her had ever been on my mind.

That was three months ago now. My relationship with Po Yi is bound with a love that cannot be broken. Her father is becoming slowly accepting of me, and I've even been allowed to spend several nights in their home. I feel well able to support Po Yi now, if she ever agrees to become my wife. That is a question that I intend to put to her the next time we meet.

Afterword

The story of *Aladdin and the Magic Lamp* is among the better known of the tales from the *Nights*, but is also one that is suspected to be an invention of the French orientalist Antoine Galland, who popularised the story in the eighteenth century.

Whether or not Galland's claim is true–that he took a Syrian scholar's telling of the tale as his source–the story nonetheless contains many elements that are found elsewhere in the *Nights*, and, indeed, has spawned imitations of its own (notably, Hans Christian Andersen's *The Tinder Box*).

At first sight, there doesn't appear to be any obvious moral to the story–Aladdin, a layabout who makes no effort to help his parents, comes upon a great fortune through no apparent effort of his own. Despite several trials and setbacks, he gains possession of everything that he desires, even extending to the hand of the emperor's daughter.

Aladdin uses cunning and resorts to the charm of a magic lamp to achieve his ends, even taking the lives of the magician and his brother along the way. These are not traits that might normally be thought to justify great reward, yet this is precisely what results for Aladdin.

This apparently unfair outcome isn't uncommon in the *Nights*–in other tales, folks who lead gentle lives fall prey to great hardships. Perhaps the teaching here is that justice doesn't always come in the earthly life, even if it is ultimately to be found in the heavenly realm.

However, Aladdin isn't totally without virtue. When he learns the lamp's secret, he does not insist that he is given everything he wants right away. He looks after the interests of his mother, and he gives generously to the poor. We are told that he is gracious before the emperor, is a brave warrior, and is one who stays faithful to his wife. Those whom he kills have done him wrong, and to grant them the right to continue their trickery would be to invite probable destruction for himself and for the worthy ventures that he'd embarked upon.

The story's morality may then best be understood by considering the symbols and archetypes contained within it. A world of untold luxury is one that comes to a person who finds peace in the heart–not the type of gold or precious stone that is mined from the earth, but the rare beauty that comes from within. Similarly, being united with a princess can be interpreted as finding unity with the higher Self–the pure heart that is the core of every person.

Aladdin undergoes a great transformation when his alleged uncle introduces him to the world. As if undergoing a rite of passage into adulthood, he is taken away from his mother and far from the safety of the city that he knows, then is left for dead when the magician takes leave of him.

He risks his life to catch a glimpse of the beautiful princess Badroulbadour, whose appearance in the baths excites a passion in him that he hadn't hitherto known. At least one version of the story tells that Aladdin had thought all women to be like his mother until he first set eyes on Badroulbadour[11], clearly indicating that this was his moment for coming of age.

There are two jinn mentioned in the story, one of which is all but forgotten about until it is summoned in desperation. If the genie of the lamp leads Aladdin to the riches of the heart, then the genie of the ring is his rescuer and the rock that he can call upon when he is at his wits' end.

Both jinn act as spiritual guides of a sort, but both have their boundaries (not profaning the honour of his

---

[11] Dawood, N. J. (translator) (1954) *Tales from the Thousand and One Nights*, Penguin.

mother in the case of one; not having the power to undo what is in the gift of another genie in the case of the slave of the ring).

Throughout the story, deceit, disguise, and evil scheming all seek to undo Aladdin. The emperor's clever adviser wants to put him in his place too, especially being driven by jealousy for his son. However, Aladdin navigates his way around all the lies and traps that are set for him.

When he becomes a man, he does not act impetuously, but chooses this moment, plans carefully, and waits patiently. He has the foresight to win the favour of the people–an initiative that ultimately spares him his life. He knows how to use tact and diplomacy, and uses charm and courtesy to endear others to him.

Perhaps some of these may be traits that he learned from his "uncle". However, unlike the magician–whose intentions are wholly selfishly driven–when he becomes a man, Aladdin shows maturity, magnanimity, and resourcefulness.

Despite his failings, Aladdin emerges as being a worthy pretender to the emperor's throne, and one who we–like the people who laud him–might come to admire.

Scheherazade's story

There once lived a great king, who was loved by all the people of the Sassanid Empire, over which he presided. His dominion stretched from Persia to China, crossing the mighty Ganges, and embracing the cloud-piercing slopes that are known as the Himalaya.

When he died, the king's two sons succeeded him, each ruling over half of the dominion that was once his kingdom.

The eldest of the two brothers, Shahryah, had a wife whom he loved dearly. He plied her with jewels, and made sure that she wanted for nothing.

However, it happened that Shahryah came to learn that his wife had been unfaithful to him, and in such a manner that he felt obliged to put her to death. This he commanded his chief vizier to execute, while it deeply troubled his soul to do so.

The king resolved that all women must be devious at heart, and he determined that the world would be a more peaceable place were there fewer of them.

He then set about a scheme that involved taking a new bride every night, then having her put to death the following morning. It was the sorry task of the chief vizier to seek out these women, then to ensure that the king's order was carried out the following day.

The king's behaviour caused great distress in the kingdom. No parent would know whether their daughter would be next to be taken. The love and goodwill that the people had once shown for the king was soon replaced with fear and contempt.

The chief vizier himself had two daughters, Scheherazade and Dinarzade. Dinarzade had no particular charms to distinguish her from other women, but her elder sister excelled in her studies in philosophy, literature, music, and medicine. Quite apart from her great intellect and wit, Scheherazade was blessed with remarkable beauty.

One day, Scheherazade approached her father with a request.

"My dear father, might it please your heart to grant me a favour?" she began.

"Assuredly, my dear daughter," replied the vizier. "Whatever you wish will be my pleasure to provide, given that it is within reason."

"My desire is to see our kingdom rid of our king's practice of sacrificing the brides that are forced to entertain him," Scheherazade continued. "It is my deep desire to be presented by you as one whom the king might call to his palace."

"Have you given leave of your senses?" cried the vizier, not attempting to disguise his obvious distress. "Surely you know by now what fate awaits you?"

"Yes, my father, I know that very well," Scheherazade returned, "But should I fail in my mission, that will be an honourable death for me."

"Consider then the task that I must face, being the one who must command the execution of my own daughter!" her father answered. "How can you allow such grief to come upon our family?"

Scheherazade repeated her request, begging her father to give her what she desired. Seeing that she was adamant, the vizier eventually agreed to offer his daughter to Shahryah.

When he came to the palace the following evening, the vizier informed the king that he would bring his own daughter to satisfy the king's pleasure the following night.

"Do you not know what fate awaits your daughter?" questioned the king. "Though she is your own kin, I will not spare her the ending that has befallen many before her. Should you fail to carry through my command, you will pay with your own head!"

The vizier returned home to tell his daughter to prepare herself for her meeting with the king. Scheherazade thanked him for honouring her request, seeming to be overjoyed that the king was ready to see her. "Do not be overcome with grief, my dear father," she urged the desperate man who stood before her. "I promise that you will not regret your decision."

Later, Scheherazade spoke privately with Dinarzade. She told her that she was to be made a bride of the king, and that since it would be her last night, she would beg him to allow Dinarzade to share their chamber. Dinarzade willingly agreed to join in her sister's plan, providing the king gave it his blessing.

"If you are permitted to join us, wake me one hour before dawn," Scheherazade advised her sister, "And ask me to tell you one of my charming stories. By this means, I intend to bring about an end to the killings that are terrorising our kingdom!"

When Scheherazade was bought to the palace the following evening, the king was astonished by her beauty. Appearing troubled, Scheherazade begged that the king allow her sister to be with her in their chamber for her final night. Temporarily moved by her tears, the king consented to her strange request, and Dinarzade was soon brought to the palace.

After reclining, Dinarzade woke Scheherazade just before dawn, then asked her to relate one of her stories, as had been agreed. And so, Scheherazade began to tell one of her favourite tales. This story was among those that are contained within this book.

When Scheherazade began her narration, the king awoke and heard her entertaining her sister. Soon, he was himself fully absorbed with the story. Scheherazade spoke so charmingly and engagingly, that it was impossible for him not to be taken in by her.

Scheherazade's story came to no complete ending, but rather begged to be continued—as though inviting a new tale. So intrigued was the king to discover how the story would continue, that he granted Scheherazade a further night to make known what would follow.

Scheherazade then related her second tale, but this too left open an ending that teased the curiosity of the king. And so, Shahryah granted Scheherazade a further night to continue with her storytelling, and in turn, another night, and then a further night beyond that. In all, Scheherazade's stories continued fully for one thousand nights, and then for one night more.

Epilogue to Scheherazade's story

During the time that she related her tales to Shahryar, Scheherazade bore the king three sons. After many moons, the noble woman at last approached the feared ruler, begging him that he might permit her to request a favour.

Bowing down in front of the king, and kissing the floor before him, Scheherazade began: "O mighty king, my esteemed master, I have now for one thousand and one nights related tales of ancient lore, adventure and wisdom. Might my Lordship now grant me one favour?"

"Ask, and it will be granted!" replied the king.

Scheherazade again prostrated herself, kissing the floor before the king. She then requested that her nurse bring her three children to her—one who could now carry himself without support, one who was still crawling, and one who suckled at the breast of his nurse.

"These are our dear children," Scheherazade continued. "I beg Your Majesty to spare my life, that I might be a good mother to them."

The king smiled, and responded warmly, "I have loved you before the birth of the first of our children. Your wit and eloquence, courage and kindness affect me deeply. You have taught me to revise my opinion of womenfolk, and I have repented my former impudence before Allah."

Scheherazade then kissed the king's hand, swearing her allegiance to him, and accepted his embrace. Soon, the king invited Scheherazade to be his bride, and a glorious wedding was arranged.

The king commended his vizier for raising such an upstanding daughter, and granted amnesty to all women. For thirty days, the people of the kingdom ate at the king's expense, and he gave generous alms to the poor.

Scheherazade and Shahryar dwelt in harmony until they were called to meet their true master—the Great Annihilator and Creator, The One who is beyond all time and space.

Stand-up

I've lived in Brighton since I finished my studies at Oxford. My family comes from West London, where my parents still live. My father practices as a barrister, and has become something of a pillar in his community. He even served as an MP for a while, but in common with many in his party, he lost his seat at the last election.

My parents castigate me for what they see as my wasting my education. They put me through St Paul's, one of the best independent schools in the country, before funding my stay at Oxford. "You should get yourself a proper job, Shilpa," my mother is always telling me, "Not keep playing around with this silly comedy thing that you're doing."

She's referring to my stand-up routine. This gives me a great buzz, if it doesn't earn me enough to pay the rent. I subsidise what little I get from playing the circuit with a small income from teaching yoga. Maybe one day I will get a "proper job", as my mother calls it, but for now I'm happy working at what I enjoy, and having the freedom to spend most days as I wish.

When I'm not teaching, my usual routine is to spend an hour in the morning practising my yoga. When the weather allows, I like to go down to the Pavilion Gardens, where I perform my contortions and stretches under the watchful gaze of the statue of the Prince Regent, which proudly stands in front of the exotic palace that was once his luxurious seaside retreat.

You meet all sorts in the park—Brighton has always been popular with day-trippers, but it's also a great magnet for students wanting to learn English, and the business types who pack into the various hotels and conference halls along the seafront.

One such recent visitor took particular interest in my deft movements one morning. This suited man watched me initially from a distance, taking his time before offering his opinions on my workout. "Nice legs!" he shouted. "Do that again—the one where you knot your leg behind your neck!"

I could see that he was chuckling to himself, obviously enjoying the spectacle of a young woman twisting herself into what I suppose he thought were suggestive poses. I carried on with my routine, unaffected by his lewd remarks.

The man seemed in no rush to move on. When I finished my stretches, I made for where he was standing, and curtly enquired whether he'd enjoyed watching my routine. I wasn't bothered by what he might say, knowing that I was very capable of asserting myself and responding with a pointed comment or two if that were needed.

The man appeared a little abashed, but repeated his observation about my suggestive moves. "Take this as a compliment, babe," he went on, his puerile smile not showing any sign of fading. "There's nothing wrong with a beautiful woman strutting her stuff in public, if you want my opinion."

"I don't want your opinion!" I replied sternly, "And don't call me 'babe' either!"

I asked him what he was doing in the park, and he told me that he'd decided to take time away from a conference that he was attending, which he said was boring him. "It's too bloody hot in that place," he added, "Much better to be out here, watching you wiggling your backside!"

"You think you're quite a smart arse, don't you?" I continued. "Hasn't it ever occurred to you that some of us 'babes' quite like sizing up guys like you from time to time?"

He seemed taken aback by my forthright approach, but this appeared to encourage him to want to pester me further. I said that, since I had a little free time, I was happy to chat with him for a while, and we walked across to sit down on a park bench on the other side of the pavilion.

"Tell me what you do," I asked the man, whose name I learned was Shiraz.

"I run a building firm," he replied. "Tough work, not for pretty girls like you."

"Do you have any 'pretty girls' on your payroll?" I asked, adopting a sarcastic tone.

"Sure we do—one of them runs the payroll, others we employ to type letters, make coffees for clients, clean the directors' cars, and the like. If they don't make a fuss, they'll be fine with me. If they try to be clever, they'll soon be shown the door."

I didn't know whether he was being serious, but it didn't take a genius to work out that this man was a sexist arsehole. He spoke about his three marriages as though he were telling the story of the *Three Little Pigs*. All of them had ended the same way when his wives found out that he'd had been unfaithful to them.

I told him about my past, and how I earned my living. He seemed surprised to discover that a young woman could survive on the comedy circuit, and even more that someone of my sex could actually be funny. He was dismissive of the better-known comediennes that I mentioned, claiming that they didn't have the edge that he thought most men had. For guys, he professed, humour came as a natural talent.

"Maybe you'd like to come and see me tonight?" I offered. "I'm doing a gig at *The Quadrant*, a bar down near the clock tower in the centre of town."

He claimed that he was too busy to honour me with his presence, making an excuse about his need to network with other construction industry bigwigs at the conference. But I repeated my challenge, baiting him by suggesting that he was afraid that I might single him out to be embarrassed in front of a jeering crowd. "Well maybe," he eventually conceded.

"You don't seem to have a very high opinion of women," I ventured, making the most obvious of observations. "No job sounds as though it's good enough for the women in your company—other than those that involve pushing papers, boiling kettles, and taking dictation. Maybe you should see how one or two of us might try out on site?"

Shiraz laughed, but collected himself before responding, "They stand no chance! Construction involves tough physical work, and women just aren't made for that. Besides, they'd be constantly breaking down at all of the taunts the lads would throw at them."

I replied that one of my friends was a surveyor, and that she was more than capable of batting back the ignorant snipes that used to greet her when she went on site. As for physical ability–well, rising from my seat, I challenged Shiraz to see if he could wrestle me to the ground.

"Oh no," he protested, "I couldn't hurt a lady!"

"You won't get a chance to hurt me!" I teased, urging him to try to knock me down.

"You're scared that I'll make an idiot of you, aren't you?" I joked. "Come on, strongman, I'm ready for you!"

My words must have touched his pride, since he responded by taking off his jacket, then came toward me to face the challenge.

We each stood our ground for a moment, exchanging steady stares that made known that both of us felt comfortable facing our opponent. Then, in an instant, I engaged him in a corner drop throw, propelling him into a back somersault that left him laying flat on the ground.

I then crouched behind him, bringing him into a chokehold, though stopping short of sucking the air from him. "Not strong enough are we, eh? Just make sure that you don't mess with me!"

I helped him to his feet again, and then we both resumed our places on the bench.

"You're not bad for a girl!" he conceded.

"Vous commencez à savoir ce que je suis sur!"

"What did you say?" he responded.

"Sie beginnen zu wissen, was ich bin!"

"Say that again?" Shiraz demanded.

"Stai cominciando a sapere quello che sto!"

"I don't get it!" He replied, admitting his ignorance, and seeming to be increasingly frustrated with my happy game of poking fun at his disadvantage.

It means "You're beginning to get the measure of me!" I eventually explained. "I spelled it out in French, German, and Italian, just so you could get the message!"

He seemed impressed that I was a linguist, as well as being accomplished in the martial arts. I went on to tell him about the two degrees that I'd earned at Oxford—my bachelors course in History and Politics, and my master's in Literature and Arts. I described some of my achievements as one-time Vice President of the Student Union, and listed some of the trophies that I'd snapped up when I was a member of the University's squash club.

Shiraz was unable to offer any triumphs to compare with my own. Even his appointment as Managing Director of his construction firm hadn't come about through hard grafting or raw talent, but since his father had owned the business, and then passed on his day-to-day responsibilities to his son.

"The guy that owned this place thought that he was a bit of a superstar too," I offered, aiming a nod in the direction of the pavilion. "All those fancy domes and turrets, each fashioned like architectural gems from the Orient–these weren't just fancy whims of an architect, but were meant to wow the punters. The lavish banquets, the music that played, and the stories that were told night after night–the prince expected everyone that he brought here to be impressed by what he'd created. But most of them ended up loathing him."

I went on to sketch out the shady biography of the Prince Regent, making reference to his disagreements with his father, and his doomed relationship with the German princess, Caroline.

"He thought that he pulled all of the strings," I continued, "But when he quickly fell out with his queen, his wily wife refused to agree to a divorce. They both had their affairs, squandered money, and tried various means to outwit each other. In the end, neither was a victor. Perhaps if they'd made an effort to recognise that each had something to give the other, things might not have turned out so dreadfully for them."

My relating of this unglamorous period in British history caused Shiraz to reflect on his own dealings with his former wives and employees.

"Sometimes I've regretted the way that I treated my wives," he admitted. "I used to see my arrogance as some sort of virtue, but it cost me dearly when my wives filed for divorce. After my third wiping out, I had to rethink my attitude."

"What did you get out of treating your women the way that you did?" I asked.

Shiraz hesitated before responding, looking for a moment as though he was ready to spill a tear.

"That took me a long time to work out," he lamented. "After my third divorce, I signed up with a therapist, who helped me understand what was prompting my behaviour. In truth, I never felt as though I'd achieved much when I was young. I struggled with my schoolwork, and never received any praise from my parents."

Shiraz paused to catch his breath. I could see from his downcast gaze that he was lost in a painful memory. I kept my distance from him, but offered what I believe were sympathetic comments and a willingness to hear his story.

"Did you come to see that your words might sometimes be more than just teasing?" I asked, keen to explore how far the therapy had taken him.

"Perhaps not as strongly as I might," he confessed. "I can see that some of the people who work for me were badly hurt by how I treated them. Some even quit their jobs, claiming that what they saw as my bullying had turned them into nervous wrecks."

"My chiding of women was never meant to hurt," he went on. "I've always believed that I was not being serious when I engaged in a little ribbing. It's just that for me, women have always been an easy target."

At this point, several tears did begin to well up in Shiraz's eyes. He seemed momentarily remorseful, but admitted that he had some distance to go before he was cured of his old habits.

Our conversation then turned to lighter matters, before I realised that I would need to leave Shiraz to continue his musing, as I had a yoga class to run within the next hour.

Before I left the park, I challenged Shiraz to another wrestling game. He chuckled at my offer, but said that he was still nursing his bruises following our last tomfoolery on the grass. I backed away from the bench, wishing him well and teasing him about his cowardice to not face up to me, then turned and broke into a determined trot back to my studio.

৵৽৻

I hadn't expected to see Shiraz again, but he crept into the upper bar at *The Quadrant* that evening, a short time after I'd started my gig. I decided to put on the glitz for this performance, steering away from the shabby top and jeans that I usually sported for such occasions. My spider web sheath dress glittered with its one thousand or more sequins—each one of them sewn on by myself.

The gig had attracted a good crowd, and I quickly settled into my regular patter of casual observations, contrived punchlines, and rude jibes at audience members. I quickly deflected the odd heckler, and galloped my way through my twenty-minute routine. For that particular performance, sexist jokes aimed at men were the order of the day.

When my set was over, the appreciative crowd treated me to a standing ovation. Bowing to acknowledge their cheers, I then made my way through the crowd to the back of the room, where Shiraz was trying his best to avoid my notice.

"You were amazing," he offered, without waiting for me to speak. "I've not seen an act that's as polished as that for a very long time. And hats off to you for the way you dealt with those hecklers!"

I thanked Shiraz for his sentiment, and invited him to share a drink with me. He was much less animated than he had been earlier, and admitted that he'd been grateful that I hadn't called for his participation during my act, worrying that I might have made him the butt of some of my jokes. I told him that I thought I'd caused him enough mischief earlier.

We clinked our glasses, offering a toast to what had been an interesting day. Turning to cheer on the next act, we each slowly supped on our beer.

As the gig was drawing to a close, I asked Shiraz whether he was going to make a fresh effort to show respect to all of his staff, whatever their gender.

"I'm set on it," he assured me. "Our conversation today has been the best therapy that I've had in ages. You really caused me to stop and think—to go inside

myself. No one that I know has your level of perception, nor the ability to apply what they know so well.
I'm indebted to you, Shilpa, and I offer you my word to
be a better person from now on."

I thanked Shiraz for his honesty, and passed him
my mobile number, inviting him to catch up with me
when he was next in Brighton.

"Maybe I could teach you a few yoga moves next
time you're in town?" I teased, as we prepared to leave.
"Make sure you bring your leotard next time you go
for a wander in Pavilion Gardens!"

"I'm sure that I'll be back for more!" he promised,
kissing my hand, and bidding me goodnight.

Afterword

Who is Scheherazade? This is a question that's vexed
many commentators of the *Nights*. For some, she is a
prototypical feminist; for others, a cunning *femme
fatale*. Then again, she is a survivor, telling stories to
prolong her life–in much the same way that life itself is
sustained through narrative; indeed, is perhaps no
more than one long story.

The heroine of the *Nights* is at once a narrator, an
advocate, and a seductress. She succeeds in changing
the balance of male-female politics–through careful
planning, intelligence, and control.

Scheherazade puts her knowledge to good use. All of the stories that she relates are ones that she has learned, not ones that she spontaneously creates. They are intricately and cleverly woven together, easily hypnotising the king, and treating him to an extended education in morality and the ways of men.

She is the archetypal storyteller, captivating her audience in the same way that the Nobel Prize-winning author Elias Canetti describes the skill of a storyteller whom he once observed demonstrating his craft in Marrakech:

"[He arranged words] in a rhythm that always struck me as highly personal. If he paused, what followed came out all the more forceful and exalted. I sensed the solemnity of certain words and the devious intent of others. Flattering compliments affected me as if they'd been directed at myself; in perilous situations I was afraid. Everything was under control: the most powerful words flew precisely as far as the storyteller wished them to."[15]

Scheherazade's story doesn't portray women in a universal way–sometimes stereotypes are represented, at other times women are shown to be resourceful and resilient, and at others, the role of heroine is emphasised.

---

[15] From Elias Canetti (2012) *The Voices of Marrakesh: A Record of a Visit*, Penguin, p 78.

She shows Shahryar that not all women are alike, and that not all are unfaithful to their husbands. So too, the necessity for men and women to complement each other, for their mutual support and sustaining, clearly comes through.

Some have suggested that Scheherazade was a historical character, even being–or at least emulating–the biblical Esther. Both are women who were advocates and saviours for their sex. However, Scheherazade is also a universal woman–she speaks Arabic, has a Persian name, and her stories often display an Indian narrative style.

For me, Scheherazade is primarily an exemplar of someone who commits to doing what she believes is right. She makes use of her education, but is deeply perceptive too. She stands up to oppression, but maintains an air of mystery; she is cunning and at times devious.

The vizier's daughter is clever, confident, and courageous–knowing that she risks her own life, as well as the misery of her family, if her mission fails. However, she is certain that presenting herself to the king is the course that she must follow. If she holds back, there is no other who will follow her, and so no hope for the king's killings to cease. She knows her gifts and is ready to serve.

With so many fine qualities to recommend her, Scheherazade is the perfect match for Shahryar, and is perfectly suited to become queen of a great nation. The legacy of tales that she related continue to enchant and inspire to this day.

ACKNOWLEDGEMENTS

I would like to thank Heather McDonald for her kind assistance with editing and proofreading my original manuscript, and James Cheung, for his expert critiquing of *What am I bid?* My thanks are also due to Karin, Frank, Kate, Barry and Jan for allowing me to stay in their homes, where I was able to find the inspiration and peace to write. My muses and writing companions–Whiskey, Emi, TJ, Tatty and Nelson–deserve credit for their various helpful meows and barks. I'm grateful to Jacqueline Abromeit for help with cover formatting. The fine staff of The British Library provided exemplary service in furnishing my reading requests. Most importantly, eternal thanks are due to The Great Creator, who inspires all ideas, and bestows the precious gifts of writing and storytelling.

The classical tales that are included in this book typically draw on more than one version of each story and include some adaptations. I have consulted the English translations of Jonathan Scott (1811), John Payne (1884), Sir Richard Burton (1885), and Andrew Lang (1885).

ABOUT THE AUTHOR

Clive Johnson is a student and follower of the perennial tradition, the belief that many myths, fairy stories and faith traditions point to common truths at their heart. Clive is an interfaith minister ordained by the One Spirit Interfaith Foundation, as well as a teacher, storyteller and retreat host. He has had a lifelong interest in the power of myth and the oral tradition of story telling. Being autistic, a would-be mystic and not approaching his reflections from an academic standpoint, he approaches his writing with an open heart and a keen curiosity. He has no fixed home, pursuing a nomadic lifestyle that allows him to follow his heart. This is his seventh book.

Clive may be reached via his website, www.interfaithministry.co.uk.

CPSIA information can be obtained
at www.ICGtesting.com
Printed in the USA
LVOW08s1616021116
511368LV00008B/595/P